"I'll tell you what happened." *Darla* seethed with revulsion. "He went and got himself a filthy soul. Now he's nothing, just like Angelus. What a waste."

"Not really—a waste, I mean." *Harmony* shrugged. "Spike couldn't kill Buffy before he got the chip. He had plenty of chances."

"But he failed," *Dru* said, "over and over again, like a broken record stuck in a groove. Couldn't kill her, couldn't kill her . . ."

Not true! Spike squeezed his eyes closed and covered his ears. He couldn't block the sound of Buffy trying to kick the corpse out the door, and he couldn't block the truth he'd been hiding from himself for five years.

He hadn't failed. . . .

Buffy the Vampire Slayer™

Available from SIMON & SCHUSTER

Spark and Burn

Diana G. Gallagher

**Based on the hit television series
created by Joss Whedon**

And based on the Buffy the Vampire Slayer episodes: "School Hard" by Joss Whedon
and David Greenwalt, "Inca Mummy Girl" by Matt Kiene and Joe Reinkemeyer, "Reptile
Boy" by David Greenwalt, "Halloween" by Carl Ellsworth, "Lie to Me" by Joss Whedon,
"What's My Line?" by Howard Gordon and Marti Noxon, "Lover's Walk" by Dan Vebber,
"The Yoko Factor" by Douglas Petrie, "The Initiative" by Douglas Petrie, "Fool for Love"
by Douglas Petrie, "Out of My Mind" by Rebecca Rand Kirshner, "Crush" by David Fury,
"Older and Far Away" by Drew Z. Greenberg, "Checkpoint" by Douglas Petrie and Jane
Espenson, "Intervention" by Jane Espenson, "The Gift" by Joss Whedon, "Seeing Red"
by Steven S. DeKnight, "Villains" by Marti Noxon, "Two to Go" by Douglas Petrie,
"Lessons" by Joss Whedon, "Lies My Parents Told Me" by David Fury and Drew Goddard,
"Beneath You" by Douglas Petrie, "Bring on the Night" by Marti Noxon and Douglas
Petrie, and "First Date" by Jane Espenson

And based on the episodes of Angel, created by Joss Whedon and David Greenwalt:
"Darla" by Tim Minear, "1943/Why We Fight" by Drew Goddard and Steven S. DeKnight,
and "In the Dark" by Douglas Petrie

SIMON SPOTLIGHT ENTERTAINMENT
New York   London   Toronto   Sydney

S|S|E

SIMON SPOTLIGHT ENTERTAINMENT

An imprint of Simon & Schuster Children's Publishing Division

1230 Avenue of the Americas, New York, New York 10020

™ & © 2005 Twentieth Century Fox Film Corporation. All rights reserved.

All rights reserved, including the right of reproduction in whole or in part in any form.

SIMON SPOTLIGHT ENTERTAINMENT and related logo are trademarks of Simon & Schuster, Inc.

Manufactured in the United States of America

First Edition 10 9 8 7 6 5 4 3 2 1

Library of Congress Control Number 2004117775

ISBN 1-4169-0056-X

For BethAnn and Kathryn Slade,
fantastic Buffy fans
and Betsey's favorite nieces!

Spark and Burn

Prologue

"**I** could never trust you enough for it to be love."

"Trust is for old marrieds, Buffy," Spike scoffed. He hadn't invaded the Slayer's bathroom hoping to save an insipid, ordinary romance. The predatory fervor that had driven them together had evolved into a ferocious, noble bond he did not want to lose. "Great love is wild and passionate and dangerous. It burns and consumes."

"Until there's nothing left." Buffy glared at him, her arms folded protectively over her gray bathrobe, her chin raised in defiance. "Love like that doesn't last."

Wrong, Slayer, Spike thought. He and Drusilla had loved with a searing intensity that had lasted over a century. It had taken the raw power of his feelings for

Buffy to shred that blood-tie with Dru. Somehow he had to make Buffy understand that.

"I know you feel like I do," Spike said, taking a step forward. It wouldn't take much to rekindle the need that had fueled their passion: a look, his lips brushing her neck, his hands drawing her close. Then maybe she would stop fooling herself and admit that she loved him. "You don't have to hide it anymore."

Buffy looked away, losing patience. "Spike, please, stop this . . ."

"Stop it!"

The heavy door slammed against the wall with a sharp *crack* as Spike stormed into his crypt. He didn't pause to close it. He could shut out the world, but not the memory of Buffy begging him to stop.

"No, stop! Please . . ."

She had lost her balance and fallen, pulling down the shower curtain and hitting the bathtub. When he had tried to pin her, she'd pushed him away, not with the Slayer's strength, but with the desperation of a woman fighting for her dignity.

But he, too, had been trapped by desperation. Determined to prove that Buffy loved him, he had been deaf to her pleas.

"Don't do this, please! Please . . ."

"Buffy . . ."

The sound of his voice enraged rather than soothed her. She fought harder, but the rejection only provoked the demon inside the vampire Spike had become.

How could she not love him when he loved her with all his heart and soul?

A withered heart that doesn't bloody beat, Spike thought bitterly as he snatched a bottle of vodka and a glass from the stone shelf under the crypt window. *As for my soul . . .*

He poured two fingers of clear liquor into the glass and set the bottle on the sarcophagus. His soul—the pathetic essence of a lovesick poet—had been mercifully evicted when Drusilla sank her fangs into his flesh to drain his blood and his humanity. He had never wondered what became of it, until he found out that Angel's soul had been restored by a gypsy curse. Apparently, since Spike had no taste for Romanian maidens, his abandoned spark was doomed to drift in the ether until he was dust.

"Please, Spike, please . . ."

He had been so sure Buffy cared for him. She could not possibly have given herself so completely to someone she loathed. Even Dawn sensed that his being with Buffy transcended forbidden lust.

Dawn. Spike tightened his jaw, cursing the Slayer's younger sister, blaming her for that night's disaster. If Little-bit hadn't told him that his spontaneous, drunken tryst with Anya had hurt Buffy, he wouldn't have gone to the house to make things right. He shook his head. *But it isn't Dawn's fault I attacked Buffy and ruined everything.*

Spike gulped the alcohol, but it didn't burn his throat or blot out the memory or dull the pain. Nothing could erase from his mind the look of terrified contempt on Buffy's tear-stained face.

"I'm going to make you feel it . . ."

"Stop!"

Spike crushed the glass in his hand. He could still feel Buffy's body underneath him on the bathroom floor, twisting to escape his grip. At first the struggle had infuriated and then aroused him, reminding him of the fight that had shattered the barriers between them the first time, when they had literally brought the house down. Then, without warning, Buffy had tapped into her slayer power and sent him flying across the small room into the wall. The shock had brought him to his senses—too late.

"Ask me again why I could never love you?"

Spike hadn't asked, but he knew. The chip in his head punished him with excruciating pain if he hurt one of the good guys, but he was still a demon.

And she didn't dare trust him.

Spike shook splinters of glass off his hand.

"Uh—knock, knock." Clem stood in the open doorway. "I was just in the neighborhood so I thought, you know—there's a *Knight Rider* marathon on TV. I got hot wings!" The flop-eared demon raised a take-out bucket.

Spike barely heard him. The gravity of his attack on Buffy had staggered him again.

"What have I done? What did I do?" Confused and wretched, Spike threw his head back. "What has she done to me?"

"She done—who?" Clem asked.

Spike turned away, waving off the question.

Usually, if there wasn't anything better to do, Spike didn't mind hanging out with Clem. The harmless demon was as much an innocent as a human toddler, without guile or malice or an agenda. But tonight Clem's cheerful company, *Knight Rider*, and spicy chicken would just wear on Spike's nerves and augment his torment.

Clem was innocent, but not dense. "Oh . . . the Slayer, huh? Gosh, she break up with you again?"

"We were never together," Spike said with a casual shrug. "Not really. She'd never lower herself that far."

"She's a sweet girl, Spike. But hey!" Clem elongated the next word: "Issues."

That's one way of putting it, Spike thought.

"And no wonder with the whole coming back from the grave and what not," Clem went on. "I had this cousin who got resurrected by some kooky shaman. Oooh, boy! Was that a mess."

"Why do I feel this way?" Spike spat out the question.

"Love's a funny thing," Clem said quietly.

"Is that what this is?" Spike demanded, putting his hand on his temple as he strode toward Clem. "I can feel it, squirming in my head."

"Love?" Clem asked, puzzled.

"The chip!" Spike winced. Sometimes he did think he could feel the nasty device burrowing into his brain. "More like bits and chunks."

"Maybe a wet cloth," Clem suggested.

"You know, everything used to be so clear. Slayer"—Spike spoke through clenched teeth, striking out to his right, then his left to make the point—"Vampire kills Slayer, sucks her dry, and picks his teeth with her bones."

Clem listened in respectful silence, clutching his bucket of hot wings.

"It's always been that way. I've tasted the life of two slayers. But with Buffy—" Spike paused. Just saying her name evoked a depth of despair that threatened to destroy what was left of the dark, dangerous creature he had once been. "It's not supposed to be this way!"

Frustrated, Spike pushed over a brass bed frame. Clem flinched, but he didn't speak.

"It's the chip. Steel and wires and silicone." Spike leaned against the sarcophagus. "It won't let me be a monster, and I can't be a man. I'm nothing."

"Hey, come on now, Mr. Negative," Clem said. "You never know what's just around the corner. Things change."

Spike hesitated, then slowly turned his head. "Yeah, they do. If you make them."

An hour later Spike was on his motorcycle, roaring down the highway. He set his jaw as he left the lights of Sunnydale behind him. He was the master of his own fate, riding the winds of change.

Things would be different when he got back.

Chapter One

Spike sat in the darkness, still and silent. His was a crowded hell, and he didn't dare move for fear more of the tormentors would awaken. Some of them were familiar. Others were long forgotten or those he'd only briefly met before he gorged on their blood.

They all wanted a piece of him now.

A horde of victims taunted him with cutting words, whispered curses, or outraged shrieks. A few sobbed endlessly.

Others, mortals and monsters he had not slaughtered, had known him well or thought they did. They jabbed his tortured psyche with verbal pins poisoned by his past.

He could not escape them. He had tried, but they

had chased him across Africa, haunted the merchant ship's cargo hold, and settled now into the basement storeroom of the new Sunnydale High School.

The vengeful dead were merciless, and they infested the spark.

". . . just sixteen," a girl hissed in a coarse Cockney accent. "Too young to die."

Spike muffled a deranged laugh, covered his ears, and rocked back and forth, but the voices wouldn't shut up! They nagged him into the oblivion of insanity, finishing what he had started when he set out to get his soul back. . . .

Africa
May 2002

A full moon hung over the Serengeti as Spike stashed the stolen Land Rover in the brush and pocketed the keys. The all-terrain vehicle couldn't take him any farther, but he'd need it to get back to the African coast—if he survived the ordeal ahead. He walked into the tribal village knowing there were only two possible outcomes: success or death. Either fate was preferable to this insufferable existence as a caricature of himself.

Intent on his destination, Spike ignored the women sitting around the fires outside thatched huts adorned with hubcaps and TV antennas. He skirted old tires, mismatched lawn furniture, baskets strewn about the sand, and a man who tried to block his way.

The language wasn't familiar, but it wasn't hard to get the man's drift.

As he swept past, Spike spoke without breaking stride. "I'm not asking for permission, mate."

Whether protesting his trespass further or warning him away, the man backed off and did not follow as the vampire crossed the village boundary into a darkness the moon could not penetrate.

Spike's vampiric eyesight allowed him to differentiate subtle gradations in the lightless surroundings. The mouth of the cave appeared as a distorted shimmer in the fabric of the night. Wary of what might lurk in the demon's lair, he flicked on his lighter as he entered. There were no obvious traps, but the flame illuminated a series of primitive paintings on the rock walls. The crude pictures of mutilated men gave Spike pause, but only long enough to catch his bearings. He knew what he wanted, and nothing would dissuade him. He walked on.

Smaller corridors branched off the entry cavern, but Spike stayed in the wide passageway that led into the heart of the cave complex.

"Do you seek me, vampire?" The commanding voice echoed off the walls.

"You do the finger paintings?" Spike asked with a calculated dash of insolence. "Nice work."

"Answer me," the demon demanded.

Spike stared into eyes of blue fire set in stone. The demon's gaze burned through his flippant facade, daring him to flinch. Spike knew his only weakness was that he wanted what he came for too much, but there was no point trying to hide it.

"Yeah," he said evenly. "I seek you."

"Something about a woman," the demon said, sifting through Spike's thoughts for the truth. "The Slayer."

Spike nodded. "Bitch thinks she's better than me. Ever since I got this bleedin' chip in my head, things ain't been right. Everything's gone to hell."

The demon's eyes flared green on blue as it flexed clawed hands. "You want to return to your former self."

Spike's gaze did not waver. "Yeah."

The demon laughed.

"What?" Spike asked, annoyed.

"Look what she's reduced you to." The demon snarled with contempt.

"It's this bloody chip." Spike's temper burned. Nobody could change him, not even the Slayer.

"You were a legendary dark warrior, and you let yourself be castrated," the demon said. "Yet you have the audacity to crawl in here and demand restoration."

"I'm still a warrior," Spike insisted.

"You're a pathetic excuse for a demon."

"Yeah?" Spike shot back. The demon was a bloody idiot if it thought a few insults could intimidate him into backing down. He took the offensive. "I'll show you pathetic. Give me your best shot."

When the demon hesitated, taking his measure, Spike knew he had won the first round.

"You'll never endure the trials required to grant your request," the demon said.

"Do your worst," Spike retorted. "But when I win, I want what I came here for. . . ."

Sunnydale
September 2002

Spike squeezed his eyes shut and banged his head back against the storeroom wall. He had gotten what he asked for, and it burned hotter than hellfire.

"Serves you right for loving the Slayer, Spike," *Dru* taunted Spike from the darkness, one of many who haunted his dementia. "The pixies in my head were quite correct about that."

"It's not love," *Buffy* scoffed. "You can't love without a soul."

Yes, you can, Spike thought, *but people with souls can't love you back.*

The Slayer knew that the chip had only harnessed his killer instincts. The demon remained inside him, embedded in the empty spaces his humanity had fled, forced to feed on foul animal blood, unable to prey on the innocent, denied the means of fulfilling his savage destiny. As surely as Drusilla had changed him into a vampire of uncommon cunning and strength, the Initiative, with their heinous chip, had turned him into a demonic eunuch that Buffy could tolerate and use, but not respect or love.

He had finally gotten the message and embarked on a fool's errand to get the missing spark back.

Another hysterical laugh rumbled in Spike's throat. He bit his lip to smother it.

He had slaughtered the demon's minions and passed every torturous test devised by the guardian of disembodied souls. At first Spike's desire for Buffy had reinforced his determination to prevail against adversaries who wielded fists of fire and swords of molten metal. But as he vanquished one challenger after another and his physical strength waned, pride had fueled his resolve as much as love. *Maybe more,* Spike thought, in a burst of rational clarity.

The demon's taunts had ripped psychic scabs off old, festering wounds. The venom of ridicule was more painful than the flames that scorched Spike's skin, more potent than the sting of swarming beetles. He would rather have ended it all than failed, but he couldn't die leaving his business with Buffy unfinished. He had survived the tortures and won. But the prize was contaminated.

The instant the demon thrust his soul back into his body, he had been overwhelmed by the anguish of the damned. The physical pain he had endured to pass the trials had been excruciating, but fleeting. The emotional torture unleashed by the spark was a thousand times worse.

And the misery would last forever.

"What have you done?" A *man* wailed.

"Murderer," an *old woman* grunted. "Go to hell."

"Mommy!" A *child* shrieked.

"You'll always be a limp, sentimental fool . . ."

"Mother . . . ," Spike muttered.

His mum's elderly face, wrinkled and twisted with disgust, flashed through his mind. Spike jumped to his feet, screaming, and slammed his fist into the wall. He had been an idiot, and now he was condemned to the hell for the deranged—*Compliments of the Slayer.*

Spike had killed Buffy many times since leaving the African cave—choking the life out of her with his bare hands, impaling her with the stake she raised against him, driving his fangs into her neck—in his dreams.

"Nightmare," Spike rasped, hanging his head.

"Poor Spike. I pinched the lost boy, but you wouldn't wake up," *Dru* said. "Instead of midnight picnic parties and sweet dreams bathed in blood, you followed your heart into the nightmare."

Spike didn't have to see Drusilla's pale, exotic face to know she was pouting. During more than a century together, she had perfected the art of making him feel guilty about real and imagined slights. Indebted and in love, he had catered to her every whim, rarely refusing her anything—until the Slayer.

"Not my fault," Spike whispered.

"Naughty Spike," *Dru* cooed, becoming visible in the lightless room. Her straight dark hair skimmed the shoulders of a black gown trimmed in red. "Mustn't tell your mummy fibs. The Slayer isn't dead and buried forever and ever."

"Not my fault," Spike said again, averting his gaze. Dru despised him because of Buffy, had left him because of Buffy—and blamed him. "The Willow-witch dug her up and put the breath back in, not me."

"You *still* haven't killed the Slayer," *Adam* accused in a deep, unemotional monotone.

Spike glanced up. Dr. Walsh's monster mutt stood where *Drusilla* had been. Constructed of human, demon, and electronic parts, Adam had been another Initiative project gone awry. Spike had struck a bargain with the calculating, built-to-be-indestructible soldier of the future: He'd deliver the Slayer like a lamb to the slaughter, and Adam would remove Spike's chip.

"But you didn't deliver," *Adam* reminded him.

Spike's eyes narrowed. His plan to isolate Buffy had failed, so Mr. Bits had reneged on their deal. The Slayer had ripped out the superfreak's power supply, saving the world from the army of demonoids Adam planned to create.

But the sodding chip is still lodged in my brain.

"Get it out!" Suddenly furious, Spike lunged at *Adam* and dropped to his knees on the floor when the manufactured mutant vanished.

"The nasty blue shocks aren't the lie, Spike," *Dru* said with petulant disappointment. "And the lit'le tin soldier knickknacks aren't to blame."

"Blame for what?" Spike asked.

"Why you can't kill her," *Dru* said as her brooding countenance morphed into a perky blond in pink.

"You couldn't kill her before you got the chip," *Harmony* said. "You had plenty of chances."

Yeah, I did, Spike thought. That was why he had come to Sunny D. in the first place: to kill the Slayer.

He should have tried harder.

New Orleans
September 1997

Fuming, Spike stepped onto the balcony of the second-floor flat he shared with Drusilla. Jaw clenched, he

gripped the black wrought-iron railing. He adored Dru,
but she was in a particularly selfish snit, and he was
nearly to the point of driving a chair leg through her
cold, dead heart. The impulse was born of frustration
and would pass, hopefully before he dusted the dark
beauty who had empowered his existence.

"She bloody well better snap out of it," Spike muttered. The aromas of spiced shrimp, fried catfish, and
gumbo rose from nearby kitchens, aggravating his
craving for blood. Still, despite his hunger and sour
mood, the midnight humidity dampened his anger as
well as his white-blond hair.

At times like this he missed the old days, when Dru
could be swayed with the promise of puppies for dessert
or a new game to relieve her chronic boredom. Her
favorite was an ingenious variation of Russian roulette
played with potential victims. She feasted on the winner.

A woman's playful shriek drew Spike's attention
to the mass of humanity clogging Bourbon Street
below. The vibrant strains of live jazz and blues
streamed through open doorways as the crowd ducked
in and out of clubs. Most of the revelers held carryout
cups of liquor that numbed wary natures and dulled
senses, making them easy prey for the lazy undead
that roamed the French Quarter. Their screams were
absorbed by the blare of saxophone and trumpet,
bawdy songs, and laughter.

Across the street, a man in an LSU sweatshirt
stopped to tie his shoe. He disappeared suddenly,
yanked off his feet and into the unforgiving dark
between buildings. His friends kept walking, drinks

in hand, exchanging lewd remarks with girls in doorways, unaware that one of their mates had gone
missing.

The after-dark, anything-goes atmosphere in New
Orleans was a magnet for ravenous demons of all types,
but especially vampires. Attracted by popular myth, the
undead had infiltrated the local black-magic set and
turned an urban legend into fact. Spike had tired of the
scene weeks ago, but Dru had been too weak to move.

"We've got to move now, though, luv," Spike muttered softly. Braced for another fit of childish pique, he
turned to go back inside.

Dru lounged on a Victorian settee with red cush-
ions. One slim white arm was thrown over her eyes.
The feathered fan she clutched in her other hand trailed
on the floor. A pale gossamer gown emphasized how
frail she had become.

"You're still cross." Dru did not uncover her eyes to
look at him. She could sense Spike's moods and what was
on his mind with disconcerting accuracy. "It smolders like
hot coals just beneath the surface, waiting to be stoked."

"I'm not upset," Spike said. "I just needed a moment
alone . . . to think about what you said."

"Shhhhh." Dru dropped her arm and placed a finger
to her lips. "The fire mustn't get out, Spike. I couldn't
bear to watch my dollies burn, melting like black butter
in a pot."

Spike started to roll his eyes but checked himself.
He had to cater to Dru's warped sense of pertinence if
he wanted to make it to the West Coast before the
Night of St. Vigeous.

"No need to worry about your dolls, pet." Spike smiled to reassure her.

Dru sat up slowly and gazed wistfully at the steamer trunk in the corner. It held all the personal treasures she refused to part with, including the dolls she had stolen or purchased in shops. Only one or two had survived years of dolly discipline unscathed.

"Poor lit'le poppets," Dru said. "Nobody to pull their hair out or twist their pretty heads off or scold them but me."

"And you do it with such delightful cruelty," Spike said, trying to hide his irritation.

Shortly after Dru's health started to fail, he had given her a china doll with dark ringlets to cheer her up. Dru's attachment to her porcelain and plastic playmates had grown stronger as she had grown weaker. If he found the *du Lac Manuscript* and cured Dru's affliction, he imagined she would burn the dolls to celebrate her recovery. In the meantime, she had to have them.

"We'll take the dolls with us," Spike said, "but we have to leave tonight."

"What if you can't find a proper four-poster in California?" Dru's brow knit in consternation.

"Don't you fret about that," Spike said. "I'll take care of it the way I always do."

Drusilla took comfort in surroundings that resembled the late nineteenth century, and Spike had never failed to provide the appropriate pieces and accoutrements. He wouldn't let her down this time either, even if he had to raid a Hollywood movie warehouse to provide the desired décor.

"But it's too hot to travel," Dru complained with a languid wave of her fan. "And I don't think I'll like being in a place called Sunnydale. I see a death by sun, Spike. A morning rain of ashes and soot . . ."

Dru closed her eyes as though to swoon, but Spike knew it was a ploy. She had a tendency to overdramatize the flashes of the future she saw but couldn't interpret. He didn't take her warnings lightly, but he had more immediate concerns. The journey would be intolerable if Dru didn't want to go.

"This is a one-time-only chance, Dru," Spike explained patiently. A power vacuum had been created at the top of the vampire hierarchy, and he was going to fill it. "The Master is dead."

Dru scowled. "Killed by the Sunnydale Slayer."

"And I'm going to kill her." Spike walked over to the settee and knelt down. "No one will dare challenge the vampire that killed three slayers for fun. I'll be the new master of the undead minions, and you'll be my princess."

"I want a bird," Dru said with a faraway look. "A yellow one that sings. And a party with cupcakes."

"Done." Spike lifted Dru's hand and brushed his lips over her translucent skin. She needed to feed before they left town. "Canary, party, cupcakes."

"With fluffy pink frosting." Dru stared into space with a vacant smile. "I think I'll like being a princess."

Rising, Spike grabbed his black duster off a chair and paused at the door. "Pack your plastic people, luv."

"But Miss Edith fusses so when she's locked in the dark," Dru whined.

"A good spanking and no supper will shut her up

before you close the lid," Spike said, humoring her. "I'll be back soon with a car and a bite for the road."

Spike took the back stairs and left the building through the alley door. He headed away from the Bourbon Street festivities to scout through low-income neighborhoods. He needed an old car, one with a backseat big enough to carry a steamer trunk.

"Like that," he said, pausing in the shadows across the street from a run-down corner service station. He watched a man in a blue uniform fill the gas tank of a large sedan. A symbol of luxurious excess when new, the gas guzzling DeSoto clunker was now older than he would have liked, but it would have to do.

The man had left the keys in the ignition, and Spike didn't have time to shop around. The Night of St. Vigeous, when vampire strength was greatest, was next Saturday. Every vampire that fancied itself a warrior would be courting the newly Anointed One, vying for position, hoping to take the old Master's place. Spike would be late to the gathering of aspirants, but hardly at a disadvantage. None of the others could match his wits, skill, or daring, and none would be smart enough to realize it.

As the man replaced the nozzle, Spike started toward the station, prepared for a quick kill and getaway. He caught a lucky break when the customer went inside to pay. Sliding into the driver's seat, Spike turned the ignition key, shifted into gear, and took off.

"A no-hassle hijack for a man in a hurry." Spike grinned as he sped toward the mall to pick up something younger for dinner.

Chapter Two

For one hundred and twenty-two years, Spike had been an element of the dark. He had blended into the night as he moved through it, a shadow of devastation and death. Now darkness mocked the loneliness and self-loathing that corroded the core of his being.

It was a familiar feeling, the last emotion he had experienced as a human so long ago.

From beneath you . . .

The words whispered through Spike's thoughts. Something dreadful was coming. Or was it here? Delirious and exhausted, he couldn't tell.

. . . beneath me . . .

He stopped pacing the small confines of the storeroom and slammed his forehead against the wall, but the past could not be purged, or ignored.

"William."

Cecily? Spike turned, scanning the dark. *Or the hideous Halfrek, perhaps?* The "justice" demon, who granted the vengeance wishes of children, sounded remarkably like the woman he had once loved.

She appeared beside him. As always when he thought of his first love—which wasn't often, until recently—he saw her in the white gown with the lavender print collar she had worn the evening of their last meeting. *Cecily* studied him with detached disdain before she spoke.

"Your heart is dried up like a prune, William. It's not got a bulge in it now, has it?"

Spike's heart had once swelled with adoration, watching Cecily glide down a stairway to join a gathering of friends. He had basked in her radiance—

"Effulgence," *Cecily* corrected—

He had idolized her before she had battered his still-beating heart to a bloody pulp.

"Metaphorically speaking, of course," *Cecily* said, reading his thoughts. A decidedly unladylike sneer curled her lip. "You were nothing to me then but an embarrassing nuisance to be swatted away."

Spike could see that now. *Truth often reveals itself too late to be of any use,* he mused. In hindsight it was obvious his infatuation with Cecily had been a foolish fantasy.

"And now you've abandoned the magnificent evil you were, to become a simpering buffoon once again," *Cecily* said. "And mad as well."

"Go away," Spike said.

"Gladly." *Cecily* smiled as she began to fade. "You're beneath me."

Beneath her station and contempt, Spike thought. At the party in London, Cecily had dismissed him without mercy or concern. He had not even been worthy of her scorn. Cruelly rejected, he had fled into the streets.

"William, the bloody awful poet"—Wrapping his arms around himself, Spike had recited the lines that popped into his head as he stumbled over the cobblestones—*"skipping down the lane. Good boy, bad boy, all the sodding same."*

London
1880

Blinded by shame and tears, William ripped the poem into pieces as he rushed away from the house—and from Cecily. The torn papers fell when he bumped into a gentleman walking the opposite way with two ladies.

Scooping the pages off the street, William lashed out at the stranger as he rose to move on. "Watch where you're going."

"Or you could take the first drooling idiot that comes along," one of the women remarked snidely.

The insult smarted with truth, William realized as he tore down the street. He was a blubbering dolt, wanting only to wallow in his hurt and humiliation.

Taking refuge in an alley behind a tavern, William sat on a bale of straw and tore the offending verses into smaller bits. However, the destructive tantrum did nothing to soothe the ache in his heart. Cecily had not just spurned his affections. She had annihilated his dignity and crushed his poetic soul.

"And I wonder, what possible catastrophe came crashing down from heaven and brought this dashing stranger to tears?"

The voice jolted William from his self-pitying indulgence. Intrigued by the unique accent, he turned his head. Standing in the glow of a single lamp, the woman was a vision of angelic sympathy despite her dark gown and somber cloak.

"Nothing. You shouldn't be alone." William looked away, embarrassed by his distraught state.

"I see you. A man surrounded by fools who cannot see his strength, his vision." She moved closer. "His glory."

William stared into her wide, knowing eyes. How was it that this beautiful stranger could see so clearly what Cecily could not—or would not?

Her demeanor changed suddenly. She danced a few steps closer to him, as though addled or drunk, spouting nonsense. "That burning baby, fish swimming all around your head."

William jumped up and raised a warning finger. He had been shamed enough tonight. He would not be robbed by a daft harlot as well. "Uh—that's quite close enough. I've heard tales of London pickpockets."

The woman held his gaze and smiled.

"You'll not be getting my purse, I tell you," William said, backing up.

"Don't need your purse." She bent forward slightly, teasing him. "Your wealth lies here"—she touched his waistcoat, over his heart, then placed her gloved hand on the side of his head—"and here—in the spirit and imagination. You walk in worlds others can't begin to imagine."

"Oh, yes." Enthralled by her words and the sultry lilt in her voice, William pushed aside his unease. He had never met anyone more fascinating—or frightening. By what magic did this woman know his innermost thoughts?

"Uh, I mean, no." William closed his eyes and swallowed hard, coming to his senses as though breaking free from a spell. "I mean, Mother's expecting me."

The woman was not deterred, and he was powerless to resist her bewitching charms. He flinched as she played with his collar, but he didn't pull away.

"I see what you want," she said softly. "Something glowing, glistening. Something . . ." She removed her hand and smiled as she held his uncertain gaze. ". . . effulgent."

Her use of the word startled him. He was certain it could not be a coincidence. Were they connected somehow? Kindred spirits bound by destiny to meet in this dark London alley? A man of science would believe him daft for thinking it. It made perfect sense to a poet.

"Do you want it?" The woman's dark eyes shone with an impassioned light, promising everything William had ever dared to dream or desire.

"Oh, yes." William tentatively touched her shoulder.

The woman was a dark mystery. He sensed he should fear her, but he was done running. She reeked of immense power, and he wanted it. "God, yes."

When her angelic features changed into a grotesque visage of deformed bone and yellow eyes, he was not afraid. He held her penetrating gaze and tensed as she leaned toward him. When her fangs first pierced his skin, he experienced a moment of pure ecstasy that was quickly followed by a rush of terror and pain.

"Ow! Ow, ow!" Fear struck like a cannonball in William's gut, and his eyes widened with realization: He was dying. He struggled for a moment, crying out, but as the life flowed out of him, so did the wretched misery. As his heartbeat slowed, then stopped, he was suspended in a gray realm between being and nonbeing.

Then the salty tang of blood touched his tongue. The taste seeped into his veins, infusing him with a strength he had never imagined, whetting his appetite for more. She grabbed his hair and pulled his lips away from her breast.

"There he is," she cooed. "My very own son and bosom companion. My sweet—"

"William," he rasped. Hungry and disoriented, he couldn't break free of the woman's powerful hold.

"Sweet William." She scowled. "I don't care for it. It reminds me of posies, ashes, ashes, all fall down. You must choose something that suits a noble creature of the dark."

"Is that what I am?"

She looked past him, locked into her own thoughts.

"Poor Drusilla, all alone. Grandmother and Angelus don't want to share, and he said I should make myself a playmate. So I did."

This time the insult would not go unanswered. Pulling out of her grasp, William clamped his hand around her slender neck. The intensity of his rage and reflexes was unexpected, and he took care not to tighten his grip. "I won't be your toy, Drusilla."

"No." She smiled. "Of all the knights in all the lands I picked you and made you mine forever with a kiss."

"Forever." He released her with a nod that sealed the pact. For the first time in his short life, someone besides his mother wanted him.

Sunnydale
September 2002

"I didn't want you." Spike's *demon mother* stood in the corner of the storeroom. "I should have dashed your brains out and saved everyone, especially me, from the tedium of your insufferable rhymes and company."

Spike closed his eyes; he couldn't bear to look at the hateful ghost. She always appeared looking as she had in her final moments, wearing a nightdress and shawl, her long, golden hair hanging loose. He mustn't be allowed to forget that he had staked the demon remains of his mother with her own broken cane. As though that were worse than the vile words that had driven him to rid his existence of her.

"Just a poseur," the *demon mother* went on, "strutting about, hoping no one would see the quivering prig buried under the arrogant bravado, needing his mum or his sire or his Slayer to make him feel a man."

Spike covered his ears with his hands. Her barbs cut as deeply now as they had that fateful night, and it mattered just as much. He had changed his invalid mother so she could survive, but she had reviled his gift.

"Spend eternity listening to your witless twaddle?" The *demon mother* laughed. "Condemned to be undead forever with you would have been a horror, William. Annihilation was a mercy."

"Dawn!" Buffy called out.

Spike pressed his hands tighter against his ears. The Slayer apparition didn't come often, but he dreaded it more than the others, more than the Master or the ravenous unknown stirring underground. Every reminder of the Slayer magnified his despair by a hundredfold. Just as he had turned his mother into a demon that was nothing like the woman who raised him, Dru had changed him into a monster Buffy was unable to love.

"You wouldn't have cared except for clinging to that last lit'le bit of your humanity," *Dru* said. "The Judge saw it, didn't he? That vile pinch of a person that stole my darling Spike."

"It's not that simple," Spike protested. Drusilla's bite had robbed him of his soul, freeing him of moral qualms and mortal constraints, but the sensitivities of the poet remained, irrevocably embedded in his psyche. To mask that inescapable flaw, he had been forced to become ruthlessly brutal.

Sunnydale
September 1997

Spike glanced at the large vampire sprawled unconscious on the factory floor. The ugly brute had believed his own hype and attacked when Spike wasn't looking. Spike had snapped his fist back, hitting the charging vampire in the jaw. *Too easy to be sporting,* Spike thought. However, the hostile underlings standing around the Anointed One had gotten the point. Spike had earned his rep as a Big Bad and enjoyed living up to it.

"So—" Spike turned toward the small boy sitting on an overturned metal vat. "Who do you kill for fun around here?"

"Who are you?" the boy wonder asked.

"Spike." He kicked Big Ugly's hand out of the way as he advanced on the boy and his ragtag crew. "You're that Anointed guy. I read about you."

In the twelfth century, Aurelius had predicted that an Anointed One would be the Master's greatest weapon against the Slayer. *Apparently,* Spike thought with an internal sneer, *things didn't work out as planned.* The Master was dead, and his orphans were still plotting to kill the Slayer.

Another vampire with a goatee and a dust wish got in Spike's face, trying to intimidate him. Spike saw the uncertainty behind his cheeky stare and smiled, moving past the vamp. *The Master's boy warrior is in charge,* he thought.

"You got slayer problems," Spike said, addressing the boy. "That's a bad piece of luck. You know what

I find works real good with slayers? Killing them."

"Can you?" the boy asked.

Of course, you moronic sod, Spike thought. *That's why I brought it up.*

"A lot faster than Nancy-boy there," he said. "Yeah, I did a couple slayers in my time. I don't like to brag." He held a straight face for a second before he started laughing. "Who am I kidding? I love to brag. There was this one slayer during the Boxer Rebellion—"

He stopped short and turned, alerted by the purring growl in Drusilla's throat as she strolled into the room. She was a vision of elegance in a nineteenth-century gown and gold necklace, radiant in the gloom that permeated the cement cavern.

"Drusilla." Spike reverted to human form as he approached her. "You shouldn't be walking around. You're weak."

"Look at all the people." She stared at the motley assortment of vampires with the fascination of a child at the zoo. "Are these nice people?"

"We're getting along," Spike said.

"This one has power." Dru focused on the Anointed One. Her madness skewed her perceptions and the reality she occupied at any given moment, but it didn't dull her ability to read those around her. "I could feel it from outside."

"Yeah, he's the big noise in these parts," Spike explained. "Anointed and all that."

"Do you like daisies?" Dru asked, but the boy didn't respond. "I plant them, but they always die. Everything I put in the ground withers and dies." She hesitated, as though aware of something that eluded everyone else. "Spike? I'm cold."

Spike whipped off his black duster and placed it around her shoulders. "I've got you."

Dru smiled. "I'm a princess."

"That's what you are." Spike shivered as Dru cut his face with her fingernail, drawing blood. He paused, kissed her, and then turned to meet the Anointed One's curious gaze. "Me and Dru, we're moving in."

The announcement was met with stunned silence.

"Now." Spike moved away from Dru. "Any of you want to test who's got the biggest wrinklies around here, step on up."

No one moved.

"I'll do your slayer for you," Spike told the boy, "but you keep your flunkies from trying anything behind my back. Deal?"

The boy nodded.

"I can't see her, the Slayer." Dru's voice trembled. "I can't see. It's dark where she is."

Spike hurried back to Dru to ease her anxiety. Drusilla had been born with precognitive sight. Although he couldn't always interpret correctly her rambling explanations of her visions, the ability to foresee events of import rarely failed her. A vision that left her in the dark was the only thing that truly frightened her.

"Kill her," Dru insisted. "Kill her, Spike. Kill her for me."

"It's done, baby," Spike said, laying a hand on her chest to calm her.

Dru began to relax. "Kill her for princess."

"I'll chop her into messes," Spike promised.

"You are my sweet, my lit'le Spike," Dru said, appeased.

Spike held Dru's gaze a moment, making sure the upset had passed, then taunted the midget warrior with an impertinent grin. "So—how about this Slayer? Is she tough?"

"She's alive," the vamp with the goatee spat back.

"For now," Spike said, drawing Dru close. As they started toward the exit, he felt the goateed vamp tense to strike. Spike cast a casual glance back. "Don't try it. Drusilla hasn't had a mate to dismember for a while."

The vampire swore, but he didn't follow as Spike led Drusilla into a dark corridor lined with pipes.

"It's so damp, Spike," Drusilla complained as she sidestepped a puddle. "I'll catch my death."

"No, you'll get better soon," Spike said. Sunnydale had been built over a Hellmouth, a source of immense power he knew he could use to renew Dru's strength and vigor. "After I kill the Slayer."

"Yes, you must kill her, Spike."

"That's the plan," Spike quipped. He didn't want Dru fretting. Worry wore her down and sent her into more frequent flights of panicked raving. He wanted to avoid any unnecessary distractions while he learned the Sunnydale Slayer's habits and quirks. Every slayer had them. It was just a matter of finding them out.

"Rip out her heart and bury her deep. Or pulverize her bones and let the wind carry the dust far, far away." Dru began to glance frantically about.

"What is it?" Spike asked, not knowing whether the threat she perceived was real or imagined.

"I can't see her, Spike. My head swims with dark clouds when I try. I'm blind—like the poor lit'le mice in the story with no tails."

"You're not blind, Dru." Spike stopped. "I'll show you. Close your eyes."

"Why?" Dru frowned, and then smiled, her distress forgotten. "Is it a surprise?"

"You'll never guess," Spike said.

Their moving routine hadn't varied much the past several years. When they arrived in a new city, he found a suitable lair, stole whatever he needed to please Dru's Victorian tastes, then "surprised" her. The only modern convenience he required was a TV. He had already installed one in the corner of the warehouse he had staked out and furnished earlier. He planned to watch an old film or rerun while Dru fussed about unpacking her dolls and trinkets.

"C'mon, Dru," Spike cajoled. "You don't want to spoil it now, do you?"

"I love surprises," Dru said, closing her eyes. They popped open again, widening with terror. "This Slayer doesn't play nice, Spike. She dances with death, twirling her stakes, making dust."

Spike realized there was no point moving onward until Drusilla's rant had run its course. She was terrified of the Slayer she couldn't see, like a child fearful of make-believe monsters under the bed. That's how it was with most vampires regarding the Slayer: cold sweats and frightened whispers.

"I feel it in my bones, rattling and shaking with fever and chills." Dru stared at the floor, her fists clenched. "She'll be the end of you, Spike. Nasty Slayer." She stamped her foot as though squashing a spider.

"I'll be careful, pet." Spike drew her close and held her, hoping the bad spell would pass soon. Her concern was touching, but unwarranted. Spike had heard it all before.

Yorkshire
1880

A mineshaft is a sod awful place to be stuck, Spike thought, rubbing his chin. Lanterns left hanging on support timbers and overhead rafters were cocooned in cobwebs, and the air was chill and stale. A table and chair, shovels, pickaxes, and crates of molding dynamite were coated with black dust and grime. They had been hiding in the deep burrow for hours waiting for nightfall, when Angelus attacked him. At first he thought his grandsire had been provoked by the humorous rhymes he had composed to entertain Darla and Dru. That, he could have understood.

"You know what I prefer to being hunted?" Spike asked, standing his ground. "Getting caught."

"That's brilliant strategy, really," Angelus retorted, toying with Spike's lapels. "Pure cunning."

"Sod off." Spike, exhilarated by the new strength flowing through his veins, faced Angelus with pugnacious defiance. He had lived the demeaning existence of a gentleman without means, dependent on his mother and tolerated as an amusing sideshow by his peers. Now all that was over and done, relegated to a footnote of the past. Everything about being a vampire—the stalking, the chase, the scent of fear, the taste of blood, the kill—made him feel alive for the first time. He would never resort to cowardly caution.

Darla, looking prim and proper in a stylish hat atop perfect blond ringlets, was quite put out because Spike's murderous deeds had forced them to flee London.

Accustomed to luxury and leisure, Angelus objected to passing a day in a mining pit and preferred finesse to a good brawl. He, too, resented the peril the new bloke's reckless actions had brought upon them.

On the other hand, Spike's exploits thrilled Drusilla. She watched him and Angelus spar with a young damsel's delight, relishing his every audacious word and move. How could he appear to be less than the vicious beast she thought him to be?

"When was the last time you unleashed it?" Spike taunted Angelus. "All-out fighting in the mob, back against the wall, nothing but fists and fangs. Don't you ever get tired of fights you know you're going to win?"

"No," Angelus answered, his gaze and attitude deadly serious. "A real kill, a good kill—it takes pure artistry. Without that, we're just animals."

"Poofter," Spike scoffed.

Angelus shoved him, but Spike shoved back, driving the more powerful vampire across the wide space where the mine's underground tunnels intersected. Incensed,

Angelus grabbed an axe and snapped its head off. Before Spike regained his balance, Angelus was gripping his coat and pushing him backward. Taller and heavier, with an edge of experience, Angelus threw Spike down on an ore cart and raised the broken axe handle to strike.

For a moment Spike thought he had pushed the older vampire too far, but the Scourge of Europe stayed his hand. It wasn't an act of compassion or sympathy for a rambunctious young mate. Angelus would gladly have ended Spike's short, glorious sojourn as a vampire except that Dru adored him. Since Spike had become Drusilla's doting companion, she had stopped pestering Angelus and Darla for attention.

"Now you're getting it." Spike grinned, tempting fate with another taunt. Angelus could kill him, and that kept him alert and honing his skills. The threat of obliteration energized both of them and, once the novelty wore off, would prevent endless days from becoming endlessly boring.

"You can't keep this up forever." Angelus pulled back. "If I can't teach you, maybe someday an angry crowd will." He answered Spike's smirk with a short, derisive laugh. "That—or the Slayer."

Spike's smug smile faded as he sat up. "What's a slayer?"

Ignoring him, Angelus motioned the women to follow as he ducked into another tunnel. "There's a draft from an auxiliary shaft somewhere ahead. The locals might be guarding it, but there's a woods nearby. I doubt they'll try to follow in the dark."

"Follow us where?" Darla asked.

"The coast," Angelus replied quickly, having already settled on a plan. "I've a sudden craving for French cuisine."

Dru gasped with pleasure. "I've always wanted to take a holiday in Paris."

Spike dusted himself off and pushed back his tangled hair, but he didn't argue about the decision. He still had much to learn about the demon world, and given the revelation about a mysterious slayer, his companions still had much to teach despite their dreadfully wary ways.

"Pack of rabbits running scared," Spike muttered.

Darla's eyes flashed with disdain. "If not for your last kill, William, we'd be sitting cozy in chambers now."

"It's Spike now," he reminded her sharply. "William the Bloody is bloody over."

"And his last encore was a work of art," Dru said, gracing Spike with an admiring glance. "A masterpiece. I never would have thought of it."

"Neither did I," Spike confessed. "Death by railroad spike through the head was his idea, actually. As was the poetry recitation to set the mood."

"It was inspired!" Dru touched one hand to her breast and began to recite. "'The bloody awful stench doth linger, painting pictures in my mind. Honey and angel hearts impaled on Cupid's crooked shaft.'"

Spike had relished tormenting and killing the pompous literary critic who had humiliated him in front of Cecily, but he couldn't bear to hear Dru mangle the verse he had struggled so to write.

"What's a slayer?" Spike asked again, diverting the conversation.

"A girl who kills vampires." Angelus paused when the tunnel dead-ended by a narrow vertical shaft.

"A girl?" Spike wasn't sure if Angelus was serious or having a joke at his expense. Trying to hide his intense interest, he leaned into the dark shaft and looked up. Stars littered the patch of night sky visible above, and he could detect no flicker of firelight or waft of human scent. "An immortal girl?"

"No, slayers all die," Angelus said as he stepped into the shaft. "Mostly while they're still young and tender." Then he was gone, blending into the dark as he climbed swiftly upward.

Spike waited until they were clear of the mine and deep into the woods before he peppered them with more questions. "Where does one find these killer lasses?"

"She's everywhere," Dru whispered. "One at a time but always one. Kill or be killed and then there's another, and she kills too. That's what they do, slayers. Kill."

"Vampires," Spike stated for clarification.

"They destroy whatever evil thing happens along," Angelus said. Although brambles and bugs bedeviled their passage through the forest, his mood had lightened now that they were on the move. "Unless something gets them first."

"Which, sad to say, makes no difference to us." Darla cursed a low-hanging branch that snagged her hat, and cursed again as she yanked it free. "There's always a new one being trained to fill the vacant niche."

"Trained by whom?" Spike asked.

"Watchers," Darla explained, "from families with a long tradition of watching over the Potentials, most of whom will never become the Slayer. I've heard that those who mentor the Chosen Few keep a record of their murderous lives. There must be a library full of their histories somewhere."

"Slayer tales with happy endings," Dru said. "Nary a one dies of old age."

"Short lives, short books," Angelus added.

It was those short lives that Spike found most intriguing. Slayers were enhanced to be a match for the vampires they hunted and fought. Yet they died. Frequently, apparently.

"How many of these slayers have you killed, Angelus?" Spike asked.

"Can't say that I've ever met a slayer face-to-face," Angelus said. "I prefer not to."

"Scared, are you?" Spike couldn't resist the jab, but Angelus didn't take offense.

"I'm not foolish." Angelus stopped, his voice smoldering with caution. "Luck, as much as power or talent, accounts for most slayer deaths, Spike. A slayer's training and ability may differ, but they're all strong, quick, and driven by one purpose—to kill vampires."

Spike was not put off. "One Slayer, many vampires. The odds are not in her favor."

"They're not." Darla hoisted her red velvet skirts to step over a fallen log. "I doubt a slayer gets much rest.

The dangers and demands of defending good against all the forces of evil must be constantly wearing her down."

"Then why the hesitation to take her on?" Spike was genuinely perplexed.

"Kill one and the next in line is called," Angelus said. "There's no point in taking the risk."

The risk is the point, Spike thought, but he held his tongue. His companions did not need to know that he would never be content preying solely on those weaker than himself. Nothing less than meeting the challenge of killing an equal or superior adversary could erase the scars left from his life.

"I smell food," Dru said as they approached a clearing. "But it's foul with onions."

"An estate," Darla said. She paused beside Angelus at the edge of the woods and stared across an expanse of meadow. A mansion, backlit by a rising moon, crowned the distant knoll.

"Dru must have gotten a whiff of the stableman." Angelus gestured toward a stone barn and cottage at the bottom of the slope. A stooped man finished hanging a clean harness on hooks just inside the barn doors, then picked up a lantern and hurried past a coach toward the small house.

"I've never acquired a taste for peasant," Darla said, taking Angelus's arm. "I'd rather get a bite in town."

"With a coach and four to carry us, we can be aboard a ship bound for France before dawn. You need a new hat." Angelus plucked Darla's damaged hat off her head and sent it sailing high into a tree.

Spike was heartened by the glimpse of the impetuous rogue who Darla had fallen in love with and who Angelus tried too hard to suppress. Perhaps the old boy had just needed a bit of a brawl to rekindle his spirit of adventure.

"Is the Slayer in France?" Spike asked.

"Forget the Slayer," Angelus said. "I don't know where she is and wouldn't tell you if I did."

Sunnydale
September 2002

The Slayer was in the high school basement, looking for Dawn. And having a testy chat with a gang of spirits. A dead girl, in particular, seemed to be nursing a nasty grudge.

"I was ripped to death by a werewolf. Is that why you let me die?"

"I was screaming for help when they pulled me down through—" a *boy* interjected.

Spike scowled. They were noisier than the phantoms buzzing about in his brain, and all of them looking to settle a score with the Slayer. Annoyed, he turned on the overhead bulb.

"Hello? Not making myself clear," Buffy snapped with crisp Slayer sarcasm. "I don't care how you died. I'm sorry for your loss, but where is my sister? Dawn!"

"She's not going to hear you," the *man* said. "This place is like a maze."

"This place is ours now. It was built on our graves."

Spike rolled his eyes, exasperated by the girl's whining. The sodding ingrates didn't understand the rules. Slayers were empowered to kill vampires and other evil beasties of the down below. Saving people was a happenstance of the job, although Buffy took it more to heart than others. It wasn't her fault a few slipped through the cracks.

"Get over it already," Spike mumbled.

"All we want is for you to leave, so we can rest again."

Not hardly, Spike thought. The spirit man's tone suffered from a severe lack of sincerity. The Slayer wasn't buying his line either.

"Actually, I'm thinking all you want is to get between me and that door," Buffy said. "Who's for finding out why?"

When the fight broke out, Spike glanced at the latches securing the door. Thick steel muffled the grunts and squeals and the thud of bodies thrown against drywall and concrete. Three against one, but the Slayer was probably winning.

"You said she was dangerous." *Adam* stepped out of the shadows. "'When the big ugly goes down, the Slayer's going to be right in the thick of it.'"

Spike hadn't been wrong about that. A horde of ambitious demons had initiated one insidious plan after another in Sunnydale, and failed time and time again because Buffy was always jumping in to muck things up.

"Not the least of which was you," *Adam* reminded him. The truth, uttered in *Adam's* matter-of-fact monotone, mocked the Big Bad rep Spike had ruthlessly cultivated once upon a time. "You have a long, humiliating history of defeat at the hands of this Slayer."

"You should have taken me to France," *Harmony* chided. "Then Buffy never would have gotten the best of you."

"If at first you don't succeed," Buffy mocked the manifest demons in the corridor outside the door. "Cheat."

Spike flinched when the Slayer shook the doors. He doubted that going to France with Harmony would have saved him. He wasn't sure what could have; he didn't know at what point it had been too late.

Chapter Three

"Cockles and mussels all die, all die-o." Dru sat in the wing-backed chair, singing softly as she sorted lengths of velvet ribbon. When she found a color that pleased her, she placed it on the trunk serving as a bed table.

Spike tugged on the chains and manacles he had bolted to the ceiling. Satisfied they would hold, he glanced at Dru with a wry smile. The array of pipes running the length of the storeroom wall was a fitting contrast to the elegance of the gold-embroidered brocade canopy, pillows, and coverlets he had nicked from a local mansion. The concessions to Dru's comfort prettied up the place but didn't change the fact that they were living in a factory. On the other hand,

Drusilla's craven demonic essence was enhanced, rather than diminished, by her beauty and domestic activities. Deception was one of evil's most effective weapons.

Spike used pretense on occasion, when it worked in his favor. He had asked the Anointed One for time to settle Dru into her new home, but his feigned submission to the Wee Wonder's authority had been a calculated ploy. He wanted to avoid the St. Vigeous rituals, which served no purpose but to keep the subordinates pumped up, and he needed free time to acquaint himself with Sunnydale and the resident Slayer.

"Now where's my Blue Britches?" Dru's brow knit in consternation. Light from candles flickering in wall sconces and a Tiffany-style lamp was reflected in the burnished wood of the four-poster and added false color to her gaunt cheeks.

"Britches?" Spike asked in alarm. Drusilla thought pants unbecoming a lady and rarely wore them. "Are you still cold?"

"I can't abide the incessant chatter." Dru touched her fingers to her temples. "All the busybody little ladies and monks telling tales. The vicar spits when he's riled."

"That's just the minion masses begging St. Vigeous for a power boost," Spike said with a nod toward the door. The repetitive dirge was getting on his nerves as well. "If chanting could give any bloke the grit to kill a slayer, the Annoying One wouldn't have a slayer problem, would he?"

"There she is." Dru's attention shifted abruptly. She reached for the doll dressed in a blue suit with white ruffles lying on the bed. "Time to hush-a-bye."

Spike watched as Drusilla tied a ribbon around the doll's mouth to silence its imaginary voice. He didn't know what she heard—or thought she heard. He figured the mental mumblings she mentioned from time to time went with having a prescient mind. He was more concerned with how much weaker she had become the past few months.

"Tell you what, luv,"—Spike crossed to the chair and gently touched Drusilla's pale face—"you finish gagging the dolls, and I'll get you someone to eat."

"Someone pretty," Drusilla said with an impish smile. "Our host has no taste in people."

"Yeah, they are an ugly bunch." When Spike bent down to kiss her cheek, Drusilla handed him the doll wearing blue britches. He tossed it on the bed and paused by the door on his way out.

Drusilla reached into the steamer trunk and pulled out a doll dressed in pink. Settling back in her chair, she sang as she knotted a pink ribbon around its mouth. "Hush-a-bye, I'll make you cry, crushed by pretty lit'le horses . . ."

As he left, Spike sensed another vampire approaching and intercepted him before he entered Dru's space. "Taking a break from choir practice?"

The large vampire who had earlier challenged Spike hesitated, thrown off by his casual attitude. "The chant will be more potent at midnight."

"They always are." Spike smiled. "Just so we're

clear, mate, I don't take kindly to anyone poking around my digs."

"The one you're with—" The brute grimaced. "She's sick."

"I'm not," Spike said coldly.

Big Ugly didn't take the hint. "But you protect her instead of purging the helpless from the pack, and that makes you weak."

Spike grabbed the big vampire's coat in both fists and shoved him across the corridor into the opposite wall. The fool had probably thought an emotional attachment was a sign of weakness when he was alive, too. Spike didn't want to test the Anointed One's patience and power with a killing just yet, but he could threaten this wanker.

"Any harm comes to Dru, and no one in this factory will be around to chant at midnight." Spike released his hold and stepped back. "But if you stopped by to borrow a pint, I was just on my way out."

Big Ugly didn't stand down or let down his guard.

"I hate arguing on empty veins," Spike quipped. "Where's the best place to shop?"

"The Bronze," the vampire said. "It's a club in the warehouse district where the young ones hang out."

"Take-out teens, eh?" Although Dru could defend herself, Spike did not want to tax her strength. He started to leave and looked back at the other vampire. "Coming?"

Big Ugly didn't jump at the invitation. "The Slayer might be there."

"Bonus points for a sighting," Spike said, grinning.

Killing a slayer wasn't without risk, and the sooner he got a handle on this one's quirks and habits, the better his chances when the showdown came. Stupidity had never been one of his shortcomings. While Dru and Darla were gorging on Chinese marinated in fear during the Boxer Rebellion, he had been stalking his first slayer.

Beijing
1900

After night fell, Spike and Dru made their way to Darla's apartment to invite her along on a romp through the riot tearing through the streets. She had been in a contrary mood earlier, a variation of the generally unpleasant disposition that had taken root after Angelus left. Drusilla told Spike that an outing might cheer up their friend.

"I didn't expect you back so soon." Darla closed the lid on her jewelery case and fastened the latch. "Was the slaughter boring? It's not even midnight."

"Boring?" Spike laughed. "Not hardly. The bloody Boxers are carving up anyone that gets in their way. European merchants, American missionaries, imperial officials—makes no never-mind to them. I don't think I ever really appreciated how bloodthirsty some humans can be."

"They're religious fanatics," Darla pointed out. "Men who are driven by spiritual conviction will commit any heinous atrocity they deem necessary to achieve their ends."

"The Righteous Harmonious Fists," Spike said. The secret society's true name was an accurate description of the group's zealotry.

Darla pulled the curtain back to look out the window. "Look at them. They seethe with fanatical purpose and fervor. They glory in their war, protected by their charms, so certain the cause they champion is just."

"The Boxers were pure of purpose when they rebelled against the imperial government." Angelus strolled out of Darla's bedchamber. His long hair was damp, and the scent of lavender lingered on his skin. "Now they've betrayed their honor to preserve the dowager empress they once swore to depose."

"Angelus!" Spike spread his arms and grinned, surprised and genuinely delighted by his grandsire's return.

Angelus had vanished two years before, on the night they had massacred a band of gypsies in Romania. Angry and aggrieved, Darla had refused to discuss the irreconcilable dispute that had driven her lover away. Whatever the cause, all seemed to be forgiven now, Spike noted as Darla handed Angelus a pair of gold cufflinks.

"Where have you been?" Spike asked, curious.

"Following bodies across two continents, trying to find you." Angelus clipped the cuffs of his shirt then knotted his tie and buttoned a red vest he had pilfered from a dead Bavarian investment banker. Darla had kept the vest, his long coat, and a suit of clothes in case he returned.

"You're late, Angelus," Dru scolded. "Grandmother has been very cross."

"Actually, you're just in time," Spike said, deciding not to pry.

"Time for what?" Angelus asked warily.

Spike threw an arm around the taller vampire's broad shoulders and turned him toward the window. Something about Angelus offended his senses, a taint that he couldn't define. He dropped his arm and stared toward the distant Buddhist temple that served as the Slayer's training arena.

"I found her," Spike said. "The Slayer."

"Did you, now?" Angelus narrowed his eyes. "By accident or were you looking?"

"I sought her out, of course," Spike said. "Like I said I would."

He had searched for twenty years, but every slayer he located died before he could mount a challenge. Then Darla had gotten it into her head to tour China. They had arrived in Beijing days before an army of religious warriors began murdering any foreigners who didn't flee. A cataclysmic ambience of fear infected the city, spicing every kill, but preying on the helpless ceased to satisfy when Spike heard about a girl who killed monsters. He had tracked the Slayer to the temple.

"Then you're a fool," Angelus said. "Soon to be a dead fool. Slayers have superhuman strength and reflexes, and their skills are honed and tempered with intensive physical and mental disciplines."

"Does that mean you don't want to take a jab or two of your own?" Spike asked, though he had no intention of sharing the glory. He knew from previous discussions that Angelus wouldn't risk a fight with the Slayer. The older vampire had nothing to prove—to himself or anyone. William, however, had not yet eradicated the trauma of contempt and ridicule heaped upon him throughout his childhood, adolescence, and young manhood.

"I've got better things to do tonight." Angelus moved away from the window and walked over to Darla.

"Let's find some frightened people to play hide-and-seek with," Dru suggested. "Or perhaps we should call on the empress. She might ask us to tea."

"That sounds like a good idea, Spike," Darla said, taking Angelus's arm. "The empress won't take off your head or drive a stake through your heart."

Spike held his temper as the couple left the room and dismissed him and his bold talk about fighting a Slayer. In the two decades since Drusilla had made him, he had vanquished demons, bullied vampires, and outsmarted human mobs alongside Angelus and Darla. He had never flinched or failed to stand his ground. Yet they still regarded him as Drusilla's pet. Killing a slayer was his only hope of winning their respect.

Taking Drusilla's hand, Spike raced out of the hotel. He lapsed into a determined silence as he guided her through narrow dirt streets jammed with refugees, oxen, and carts loaded with furniture and bundles. The air was thick with smoke and ash, and they narrowly escaped being buried under a burning building that collapsed as they passed. No corner of the ancient city was free of the stench of charred flesh or the sounds of human terror.

Spike pulled Drusilla under the red-tiled portico of the temple just as an explosion showered the area with burning embers.

"It's raining fire." Drusilla stared at a small fountain in the garden courtyard and gasped when a hot coal struck the basin and sizzled out. She shrank back.

"You'll be safe here." Spike drew her toward the towering temple doors and eased her down onto a curved bench. "You'll know when she's dead—or I am."

"I'll hear the angels screaming," Dru said, giving not a hint whether that bode well for him or not.

Spike opened the massive doors just wide enough to pass through and strode into the Slayer's den. Two large statues of stylized lions flanked the wide entryway. Smaller figurines of Buddha, lions, and dragons sat on ornately sculpted wooden chests on the perimeter walls. The floor was inlaid with etched wooden tiles, and shelves carved into the supporting columns held more replicas of the revered Chinese Buddha. Red lanterns and clusters of candles cast everything in crimson light, while flames from encroaching fires singed the wooden latticework over the windows.

Spike sensed the Slayer before he saw her.

Holding a sword above her head, the slim girl charged from behind a giant central Buddha. Her movements were unrestricted by her loose tunic and pants, and she wore her long black hair woven into the single braid of a warrior. Barely a hundred pounds, with a delicate heart-shaped face, she did not look capable of hurting anyone.

Spike snaked his hand out to grab her wrist but

clutched air as the girl ducked and rolled. She ducked again when he took a wild swing at her head, and then rocked him back with a fist to the chin. He staggered, eluding the sword she was whipping around her head with the strength and expertise of a seasoned fighter.

Spike wasn't certain what he had been expecting. Perhaps, in his demonic arrogance, he had thought the tales of young girls adept at killing vampires were exaggerated. But as he stood facing the girl, he realized the stories were inadequate. Perfectly balanced on one foot with the sword raised over her head, the Slayer was as powerful and focused on his destruction as the legend had promised.

But Spike was not without his own resources. He had diligently honed his skills and fine-tuned his vampirically enhanced reflexes over the years. His efforts had been pursued with the resolve of a victim bent on vengeance and vindication. A mild-mannered man without distinction in life, he would not be one of ten thousand undistinguished henchmen in death. Underneath the insolent, carefree facade, he aspired to a greatness that went far beyond impressing Darla and Angelus. His reputation as a vampire of ruthless cunning and audacity would be known and respected throughout the world.

Starting today, Spike thought as the girl rushed him again. The sword sliced the air, missing him twice before cutting him above the eye. The sting was the catalyst that aroused the demon within. He felt his features shift into vampire form, and he took another blow that sent him reeling backward.

"Just like I pictured it," Spike said as she advanced on him again. "Is it good for you?"

The Slayer did not respond to his taunts. She lunged, kicking and slashing, but failed to connect. Spike twisted to avoid the sword, then grabbed the blade and jammed it into a massive sculpture. Forced to let go, the girl abandoned the weapon to fight with fists and feet.

Each blow Spike landed or took sent another jolt of rage coursing through his veins until he couldn't contain the power. He roared and pressed the attack, hitting her hard and hitting her again until he missed and was thrown off balance. The girl planted a boot in his back, shoved him into a wall, and pinned him with a foot on his chest.

Spike stared as the Slayer drew a stake, suddenly aware that he could end up as a pile of dust on a fat man's temple floor. As he gripped her foot to cast her off, she brought the stake down toward his heart. An explosion blasted through the latticework, sending the girl sprawling.

No matter how this comes out, Spike thought as the girl regained her feet and charged, *it was worth the risk.* Battling the Slayer and knowing he could lose was a true test of his mettle.

Spike clamped on to the Slayer's arm and slammed it against his leg, forcing her to drop the stake. As she reached to retrieve it, he clasped her wrist, twisted her arm behind her back, and held her in his vicelike embrace. His fangs sank deep into her neck, and he feasted on her enriched blood as her heartbeat slowed.

When her eyes fluttered open, Spike stared into the brown depths, hoping to glimpse the unique, dynamic spark that empowered a vampire slayer. All he saw was sorrow as she spoke a few words in Chinese, and died.

Sunnydale
September 1997

Spike stood by the dumpster outside The Bronze, smoking a cigarette. A parade of tasty teenagers wandered in and out of the converted warehouse, but he was in no hurry to hook Dru's catch-of-the-day. He had sent Big Ugly inside to scout for the Slayer, but that was only a pretext—Spike could spot a slayer with his eyes closed. He just didn't want company while he plotted the big boy's imminent demise.

"Not much light, lots of trash lying about." Spike ground the butt of his smoke under his heel and headed for the club entrance. The alley would do for a fact-finding ambush.

The bouncer ignored Spike as he breezed into the club, and the crowd clogging the area inside the door parted to let him through—not a conscious decision, but a response to the force generated by his presence. They reacted without being aware of him, like water flowing around rock.

The Bronze reminded Spike of a hundred other popular hangouts he had hunted over the years. Vacant warehouses and factories could be renovated on the cheap, and the low-life illusion created by the rough décors appealed to middle-class kids looking for safe thrills. *No risk, no rush,* Spike thought with a sweeping glance around the room.

Neon signs hung over a bar that, judging from the average age of the clientele, probably served more lattes and soft drinks than beer and wine. Movie posters, fliers, and graffiti covered the walls, and the floor was crammed with tall tables and stools. Dancers gyrated in mindless abandon to the beat of a local band. Geeks with guitars strutted their stuff on stage, parlaying a passable talent for music into a surefire girl magnet.

All of it faded into the background when Spike sensed the smoldering energies radiating from the Slayer.

Blond and tan, with a slim body packed into a lavender top and jeans, she was prettier than the other slayers he had killed. She sat at a table with a red-headed friend and an open notebook, mangling French.

"You're just not focused," the redhead said. "It's Angel-missage."

"Well, he didn't say for sure." The Slayer shrugged. "It was a maybe-see-you-there deal."

The words washed over Spike, unheard and unimportant as he studied the Slayer from angles mortals couldn't detect or comprehend. An aura of power surrounded her, generated by a core of intense inner strength. She existed in a state of spring-coiled tension—always armed, and primed to strike at the slightest provocation. Anticipation of the clash to come turned the cold blood in his veins to liquid fire.

"Guys, I'm all alone out there." A tall boy with dark hair rushed over to the table. "Somebody has to dance with me."

"Well, *we* are studying." Red, as Spike instantly dubbed the Slayer's friend, certainly knew how to throw a damper on a party.

The lanky loser wasn't having any of it, though. "Come on. One dance," the boy insisted. "You've been studying, like, twelve minutes?"

"No wonder my brain's fried," the Slayer said. "Come on."

The guitarist struck a chord that almost quickened a pulse in Spike's dead heart as the Slayer slipped off her seat. *Pretty and perky,* he thought as both girls joined the boy on the dance floor. *Fascinating.*

"I did a stupid thing last night," the lead singer sang.

Spike stared, startled by the impact of his first impression. The Sunnydale Slayer was a free spirit with a social life, not traits he usually associated with her kind. Most of the Chosen Ones lived strictly to kill vampires, and died trying.

"One step away from spilling my guts to you . . ."

I'd love to spill your blood, Spike thought. The girl danced like poetry, evoking a profound appreciation of beauty that he rarely acknowledged. Destroying her would be all the sweeter for it.

China Doll had relied on disciplined techniques of the ancient martial arts—to no avail. The second slayer had made up in raw power what she lacked in finesse. He still cursed the boy who had cut short their deadly duet in the rain.

New York
1977

The rain fell in blinding sheets, blurring the stark out-
lines of skyscrapers that rose into Manhattan's night
sky. Rivers of water flowed down the park sidewalk,
but the slippery footing and her long leather trench
didn't detract from the Slayer's form or style. She sent
Spike tumbling backward with a solid kick.

"Well, all right!" Spike exclaimed as he rolled
back onto his feet. "You've got the moves, don't you?
I'm going to ride you hard before I put you away, luv."
He dared the dark-skinned woman with a cruel grin,
but the grotesque visage of vampire ridges and fangs
didn't intimidate her.

"Are you sure about that?" She moved with a
proud slayer swagger to face him. "You actually look a
little limp and wet to me. And I ain't your love."

Nikki was old for a slayer, but Spike knew she
had survived as much by her wits as her prowess.
Every slayer had a weakness, he just hadn't figured
hers out yet.

Nikki renewed the battle with a vengeance, landing a barrage of blows Spike deftly returned. Nothing
excited and energized him more than tempting death in
a dance with a slayer. Almost a hundred years had
passed since China, but the rush was as exhilarating as
he remembered.

When Nikki went down on her back, Spike thought
it was over. After weeks spent tracking her down,
he had hoped for a more satisfying duel. She didn't

disappoint. With a surge of slayer determination and strength, she booted him backward and drove in with a fist that doubled him over. He absorbed another hit before he made his move, staying the Slayer's arm and drawing her into his lethal vampire's embrace. Snarling, he tensed to drive his fangs into her neck.

Something metal crashed and clattered behind him. Instinctively, Spike looked back to assess the threat and saw a small boy and a toppled litter basket. The child stood behind a park bench, watching with wide, frightened eyes, water running down his dark rain hat and slicker.

Taking the opening without hesitation, the Slayer threw her head back. She cracked Spike in the chin and followed through with a fist to his stomach before she flipped him.

As Spike rolled clear, he realized he had lost the advantage. The Slayer was no longer just trying to rid the world of one more vampire. She was fighting to save her son.

As he started to rise, Spike saw Nikki throw a stake. He caught it before it touched his jacket.

"I've spent a long time trying to track you down," Spike said. "I don't really want the dance to end so soon, do you, Nikki? The music's just starting, isn't it?"

Winded and soaked, the Slayer glared without answering.

Spike tossed the stake on the ground and mounted a concrete wall. "Oh, and by the way, love the coat."

The Slayer didn't give chase when he jumped off the wall into a gully and ran into the night.

"But I'll see you later, Slayer," Spike mumbled as his vampire features smoothed into human flesh and form. He wasn't upset about postponing the climax of Nikki's chapter in the continuing saga of Spike versus the vampire slayers. Being somewhat of an expert on the Chosen killers, he knew she'd come looking for him. "She won't be able to help herself."

Spike had studied slayers since learning of their existence from Angelus. The more audacious ones loved the fight, but they were often victims of their superior abilities. Believing themselves invincible or immortal, they took unnecessary chances and died before he found them.

Except for the girl in China, Spike thought with a wistful smile. He had lucked right into that one, thanks to Darla's perverse interest in religious wars, but the first kill had spoiled him. Too many slayers weren't up to the high standards China Doll had set, and weren't worth the time or effort to track them down. Most didn't survive long enough to warrant a mention on the vampire grapevine.

Drenched and hungry, Spike headed into the subway where he had taken up residence in an abandoned construction annex between stations. The underground network was a cornucopia of humanity, from runaways and derelicts to businessmen and suburban shoppers. It wouldn't take long to find someone appealing, although there was no substitute for slayer blood.

On the bright side, after his glimpse of the small boy, he knew that Nikki was a slayer with other priorities. The mission drove her with the same relentless dedication to duty all slayers had in common, but she had a rare and unusual weakness: a son and the burden of a mother's worry. The tidbit was her soft spot, one Spike was confident he could exploit.

Nikki would show up to dance with the Big Bad again. And with luck, she'd wear that coat.

Sunnydale
September 1997

Spike tightened his jaw as he watched the Sunnydale Slayer swing and sway on the dance floor. There was something disturbing about her he couldn't quite figure, an intangible magnetism he hadn't encountered before. He wasn't imagining the power he sensed in her, but some elusive factor gave him pause. Killing a slayer wasn't simply a matter of being stronger, faster, more agile, or even smarter than she was. He never talked about it, not even to Dru, but the black duster he had taken off Nikki was a constant reminder that sometimes slayers just gave up.

The meaning of China Doll's last words, spoken in Chinese, had been embedded in the sadness Spike saw in her eyes before she died. He and Dru had left the Orient to safari on the Serengeti before he finally understood. The Chinese girl had just let go of a monumental responsibility she had not sought, and relinquished a destiny some undefined force for good had given her. For a slayer, death was the only way out.

Nikki had died to protect her son.

And he had felt cheated, even though her unexpected capitulation was his own fault. The long coat had been his consolation prize.

Sometimes even the smartest vampires outsmart themselves, Spike thought. When Nikki isolated him in a subway car, he had pointed out that the son of a slayer was bound to end up dead, killed by one demon or another, sooner or later. He had meant to incite her maternal ferocity, to fuse it with her immense slayer power so she had no choice but to try to take him out, to stop him from hunting the brat. He wanted to win, but he didn't want it to be easy.

It had been a decent brawl, but when he looked into Nikki's eyes before he broke her neck, he saw surrender. She had opted out knowing her Watcher would take her orphaned son somewhere safe.

Spike was two for two, but neither of the dead slayers had quite lived up to her hype.

Judging by her appearance, the Sunnydale model was a typical California teenager who'd rather dance than learn to conjugate a French verb, and who probably lost sleep if she chipped her nail paint. Then again, few things in this world were what they seemed. He knew she had the power, but did she have the will? He'd know soon enough where this girl fit on the slayer threat scale.

Maybe three's the charm, Spike thought as he walked up to Big Ugly. Oblivious to the six-inch difference in their heights, he looked up into the larger vamp's craggy face. "Go get something to eat."

The big vampire couldn't leave fast enough.

With the bait dispatched, Spike strode over to a man within hearing distance of the dancing Slayer. "Where's the phone? I need to call the police. There's some big guy out there trying to bite someone."

Knowing something about slayer behavior, Spike was not surprised that the ruse worked exactly as he'd planned. The Slayer was heading for the door the instant she heard the word "bite." He ducked out the back way. In order to get a true reading on the girl's style and skills, he had to watch her unobserved. He hung back in the shadows, but he had a clear view of the show.

Just as Big Ugly was about to turn a sobbing girl into a meal, the Slayer grabbed him and hurled him aside. The big vampire hit the ground and rolled. He looked startled, then emboldened when he saw who had interfered. "Slayer."

"Slayee," the girl quipped.

Spike gave her points for being quick with the snappy comeback, but he wasn't going to challenge her to an exchange of verbal barbs.

The Slayer spun, whacking the big guy with her foot and absorbing his first blow. She wasn't as steady on the return punch. Big Ugly snagged her arm and sent her flying into the corrugated door across the alley. She looked a bit stunned coming off the fall, but she was on her feet and slipping by her opponent before the brute could adjust. Unable to stop his forward momentum, he smashed into the ridged door.

While the Slayer fended off the vampire, her two pals from the dance floor rushed out to save the stupid damsel Big Ugly had singled out for chow. It occurred to Spike that one of the great cosmic mysteries was why rescued victims of supernatural and mortal crimes stood around gawking instead of running away when they had the chance.

"Get her out of here!" the Slayer yelled to her friends between repeated blows to Big Ugly's fanged face. "A stake would be nice!"

What? Spike cocked a curious eyebrow. It wasn't every slayer who ventured forth without her trusty pointed killing stick. However, her punches were precise and powerful—the girl wasn't incompetent.

Red and the tall boy jumped to do her bidding and hauled the rescued girl out of harm's way. Spike had never known a slayer who had her own gang of minions.

Spike winced when Big Ugly struck the Slayer hard enough to throw her off her feet. She didn't bounce back as he expected, but lay on the pavement, staring up at the towering vampire in apparent shock and awe.

"I don't need to wait for St. Vigeous," Big Ugly gloated. "You're mine."

Bloody hell, Spike thought furiously. For a minute there, the girl's confidence and combat techniques had more than measured up to the inherent power of a slayer. The plan had been to run her through her paces, not see her done in by a giant klutz. He needed a third slayer kill to establish a record no vampire would ever match, and there was no telling where the next Chosen One would pop up.

But the Sunnydale Slayer wasn't finished. As the

big guy leaned over, she clocked him with a kick and twisted herself upright again.

"Spike!" Big Ugly urged. "Give me a hand."

At this, the Slayer snapped her head around to look. Spike stayed where he was, invisible in the shadows.

"Buffy!" The boy called the Slayer by name and threw her a stake.

Buffy? Spike almost laughed out loud. What kind of name was that for a slayer? It sounded like cotton candy, giggles, and other nauseating cuddles humans described as cute. Then the girl charged and punctured Big Ugly's heart with the stake. *Not funny or cute.*

As the big vampire disintegrated and the dust settled, Spike walked into the light, applauding her performance. "Nice work, luv."

Buffy frowned. "Who are you?"

"You'll find out on Saturday," Spike replied evenly.

"What happens on Saturday?" the Slayer asked with a nervous toss of her head.

He was blunt. "I kill you."

The Slayer just stared and let him walk away.

Stroll away, to be precise, Spike thought when he reached the end of the alley. Why hadn't she come after him? Too stunned by his bold announcement? Too tired from the fight? Worried about her pals? All of the above, or none? *Doesn't matter,* he realized. He had learned what he needed to know.

The Slayer called Buffy was quick of mind and body and gifted with a predator's instincts and responses; a better warrior, perhaps, than his two previous trophies.

Just how much better remained to be seen, but she had passed his first test.

Beating her wouldn't be easy.

Killing the two boys in the alley, however, took no time at all. They were dead and discarded within seconds, and didn't make a sound to alert the girl who had been walking with them. She was a little too tart and hard-edged for Spike's tastes, but Drusilla loved a spicy bite.

Chapter Four

Spike opened the storeroom door.

"Spike." The Slayer seemed as stunned to find him now in the Sunnydale High School basement as she had been when they first met outside The Bronze. "Are you real?"

That was a question he didn't know how to answer. He laughed.

Reality was a constantly shifting kaleidoscope of conflict in his head. Some bits made sense until he tried to latch on and they got all jumbled up again. The people getting their jollies off tormenting him had been real once. Were they real now, or were they phantoms? Maybe *he* was the phantom, a figment of cosmic imagination. The beast roiling underground, straining to escape the Hellmouth, was real. He knew that. Maybe It was the only reality, getting ready to change clothes because all the pieces didn't fit right anymore.

The manifest spirits were too fixated on self-pity to care. The disgruntled dead were brought back to seek vengeance. They were corporeal and capable of inflicting physical harm. He had forgotten about them, but they had not forgotten about the Slayer.

"Buffy—" Spike placed his hand on the Slayer's cheek. She felt real. "Duck."

"What?" She melted into his touch for a fleeting second. "Duck? There's a duck?"

The grumpy manifest man clobbered Buffy with a pipe, and she crumpled to the ground like a rag doll.

Hurt the girl. A jolt of painful self-recrimination instantly threw Spike's unstable emotional equilibrium off kilter. He backed away from the fallen Slayer, retreating into deranged denial. "No visitors today. Terribly busy."

"That rotting one's got the spine to kill her," *Dru* said when the spirit-man hit Buffy again. "But you were supposed to kill the Slayer, Spike."

"Told you to get out," the younger male spirit said, meaning Buffy.

The Slayer hadn't lost her touch, Spike noticed. She countered a pipe to the arm with a kick to zombie-man's ankle, and the decomposing wanker fell outside the doorway. Served him right. The manifest dead people said they wanted Buffy to leave, but that was a lie. They wanted to kill her.

"You promised to kill her for princess," *Dru* pouted.

"He promised to take me to France," *Harmony* huffed, crossing her arms over hot pink cashmere. "Spike kill the Slayer? That's a joke."

"Spike killed a slayer once"—*Darla* began.

Twice! Spike's battered identity flared in objection.

—"while Angelus was saving missionaries from me." *Darla* wore red, her favorite color, with bustle and hat. "What happened to that Spike?"

He's not here, Spike thought, clinging to the numbing fog that muddled truth in his mind.

Buffy slammed the heavy door against manifest man's head to shove him out of the way.

"I'll tell you what happened." *Darla* seethed with revulsion. "He went and got himself a filthy soul. Now he's nothing, just like Angelus. What a waste."

"Not really—a waste, I mean." *Harmony* shrugged. "Spike couldn't kill Buffy before he got the chip. He had plenty of chances."

"But he failed," *Dru* said, "over and over again, like a broken record stuck in a groove. Couldn't kill her, couldn't kill her . . ."

Not true! Spike squeezed his eyes closed and covered his ears. He couldn't block the sound of Buffy trying to kick the corpse out the door, and he couldn't block the truth he'd been hiding from himself for five years.

He hadn't failed. . . .

Sunnydale
September 1997

Spike swept through the side streets and back alleys of Sunnydale. It was only Thursday, two days before the Night of St. Vigeous, but he couldn't resist crashing a party and catching the Slayer off guard. Shelia, the tart he had picked up outside The Bronze the night before, had been a treasure trove of interesting facts about Buffy before Dru drank her dry.

Tonight was Parent-Teacher Night at Sunnydale High, and Buffy was in charge. *Punch and cookies meets blood and fang,* Spike thought, amused. The cultural symbolism depicting both sides of the imminent clash had a depraved appeal.

"I don't think this is a good idea," Jack—short for lumberjack—grumbled. The vampire was a tall bumpkin with a lower-than-average IQ and a childish attachment to his blue plaid shirt.

"Then why'd you sign on, mate?" Spike asked.

"'Cause the Anointed One said it was okay," Jack admitted, "and everyone else did."

"There you go, then." Spike gave the big oaf a hearty pat on the back. Jack wasn't very bright, but he was brawny and wanted to rampage.

The Anointed One hadn't been keen on speeding up the schedule when Spike first mentioned it either. Spike could tackle the Slayer on his own, so he went to the boy for help to pull off a decent massacre at the school. And truth be told, Spike could only chant "St. Vigeous, you who murdered so many, we beseech you, cleanse us of our weaknesses" for a couple minutes without gagging. He certainly wasn't about to stand round for three days begging some long-dead crusader for a power he already had. The baby boss and crew had needed a bit of convincing, especially after they found out that he had blabbed the plan.

Spike paused on the edge of the campus, scanning the front of the brick high school. There would be no sneaking in and sneaking up on their victims on his watch. When he arrived on the scene, he wanted the Slayer to know he was there.

Carmen, a female with long black hair, stepped up beside him. "Why are you so sure the Slayer will be surprised?"

"Was I talking to myself last night?" Spike asked. The Anointed One's motley horde confirmed his theory that there was an unlimited supply of vampire minions because lazy, moronic vampires fed on the easiest prey they could find—other not-too-swift slackers. They never risked anything. "I told her I'd kill her on Saturday."

"What if she doesn't believe you?" Jack asked.

"She will," Spike insisted, losing patience, "when she finds out that Saturday is the Night of St. Vigeous. I'm sure her Watcher has the book that explains about unholy ones getting all worked up into a fury that culminates in a savage attack. The brainy ones all do."

"But it's Thursday." Jack frowned.

"Exactly. Surprise!" Spike dispersed most of the vampires to vantage points around the school and at the exits. Then, with Carmen, Jack, a vampire he had nicknamed Goatee, and another male, he set his sights on the large, multi-paned cafeteria window. The lights were on, and he could see people milling about inside. Chances were that Buffy, the principal's designated hostess for the bash, would be there or nearby.

As Spike crossed the grass, he wondered again how the Watchers' journals portrayed him. Since he had done in two slayers, he had no doubt that someone had written something. Did they refer to him as Spike? Did they know that the name William the Bloody had nothing to do with being a ruthless killer? Someday he'd have to check it out. Tonight he had more urgent business.

As Spike leaped toward the window, the cafeteria alcove went dark. Glass and wood splintered as he crashed into the room, and people scattered, screaming. He landed in a crouch and as he stood up flipped a table over. His four henchmen were arrayed behind him.

The Slayer, Spike was pleased to note, was shocked to see him. She stood paralyzed on the far side of the cafeteria, looking Miss America, peaches-and-cream wholesome in a green top, white skirt, and blue sweater. Was it possible, he wondered, that her Achilles' heel was slayer denial? She wouldn't be the first to reject her destiny. *Or the last,* he thought. Tomorrow morning another girl would call herself Slayer.

"What can I say?" Vamped out and feeling cocky, Spike smirked. "I couldn't wait."

Spike saw Buffy's gaze dart to the chair, and he charged as she lunged to grab it. The girl was quicker, flinging the chair and taking him down before she took the hand of an older woman and ran.

Irritated, Spike grabbed a man with glasses who had the misfortune of being within reach. "Nobody gets out! Especially the girl."

The Slayer called out from somewhere down the hall. "Everybody this way! Come on! Come on!"

The minions fanned out to kill and feed.

Spike hauled his catch into the hall to take stock of the initial chaos.

A girl shrieked, and another girl yelled, "Hey!"

Although Spike's hearing was acute, it was difficult to differentiate and pinpoint the location of specific voices. There was much running, garbled exclamations, and screams throughout the building.

The goateed vampire, who resented the hell out of Spike's takeover tactics, ran up to Spike in the corridor. "We cut the power. Nobody got out."

"And the Slayer?" Spike asked, still holding the terrified black man by the front of his shirt.

"She either went that way"—Goatee pointed down the hall past Spike, then in the opposite direction—"or that way. I saw two others."

This time Spike couldn't hold his temper. He swung his hostage around and glared at the vampire messenger. "You don't know?"

Goatee didn't answer.

Spike wasn't as angry with the subordinate as he was with himself. The Slayer had been surprised when he popped in unannounced, but she hadn't been intimidated. She had taken quick, definitive action and escaped his opening gambit. He, on the other hand, had misread her initial reaction and underestimated her resourcefulness, fatal mistakes if he made them again. He wouldn't, but he still had a major mad to vent.

He turned on his hostage.

"I'm a veal kind of guy. You're too old to eat." Spike released the man's shirt and promptly broke his neck, adding, "But not to kill."

Goatee stared, yellow eyes wide, his jaw slack with disbelief. Apparently, Spike noted with satisfaction, being mean and ornery had finally made the proper impression. *Good,* he thought, *because one of these days, the local undead dolts will be taking orders from me or dusting Sunnydale windowsills.*

"I feel better," Spike said. And he did. Not as good as he felt when he used railroad spikes, but better than a minute ago. The black man's senseless death had been quick, perhaps even painless. A railroad spike produced a rhapsody of terror and agony—and made him think of Cecily, which always made him peckish.

Many times since killing Cecily's gentleman friend for the unkind, public critique of his poetry, Spike had regretted not killing her. He had been too infatuated with Dru to bother, but Cecily's end might have erased the cruel words she had used to devastate him.

"You're nothing to me, William. You're beneath me."

The words had burrowed deep into his psyche, and lay there like a dormant disease waiting to ravage the bits of William he had salvaged and woven into Spike. Killing girls who killed vampires took some of the sting out. He didn't know or care why.

With Goatee following a respectful ten paces behind, Spike strolled the corridors. He would find the Slayer or she would find him. There was no way out of the building.

"Slayer!" Spike called. His tone was deliberately condescending, the words a verbal slap. "Here, kitty, kitty."

The halls were eerily quiet, with no power and everyone hiding, holding their breath, trying so hard not to make a sound a vampire might hear. That was pathetically amusing, but Spike had come to fight and he quickly bored of the cat and mouse game.

"I find one of your friends first, I'm gonna suck 'em dry." His tone hardened as he trawled to draw the Slayer out. "And use their bones to bash your head in."

He hesitated, wondering if he had heard a thump or if his mind was playing tricks.

"Are you getting a word picture here?" Spike asked as he walked toward the library. No one answered.

"Spike!" Goatee shouted, then added in a whisper, "Listen."

Spike took a few steps back, his gaze drawn to the soft thudding noises above. "Someone's in the ceiling," he sing-songed. Another thump sounded behind him. Spotting Jack ramming his shoulder into a closed classroom door, he ambled over and fixed the dimwit vampire with a questioning stare.

"Uh—the door is solid," Jack stammered.

"Use your head," Spike suggested. Suddenly fed up with incompetence, he grabbed the back of Jack's neck and slammed him face-first into the firebox on the wall, breaking the glass. Spike yanked an axe free and shoved it at the startled vampire. Jack immediately set about hacking through the classroom door.

Goatee was down the hall, trying to break through a second door into the classroom.

Spike stormed by him and shouted at Carmen as she entered the hall. "You! Come with me." The female vampire dutifully fell into step behind him.

Back in the cafeteria, Spike heard the Slayer's telltale thuds overhead, but he couldn't lock onto her exact location. The girl had freedom of movement unencumbered by walls in the open ceiling crawl space. He picked up two struts from the broken table, tossed one to Carmen, and then jammed the end of the makeshift pike through the ceiling. Carmen followed his lead, but the struts went through the ceiling panels into air.

A familiar throaty roar brought Spike up short. When he turned to identify the source, he couldn't contain his surprise. "Angelus!"

"Spike!" The grinning Angelus had the Slayer's lanky boy follower in a headlock.

"I'll be damned!" Tossing the strut aside, Spike rushed to embrace his old friend and mentor. Decades had passed since they'd last met.

"I taught you always to guard your perimeter." Angelus shook his head, chiding Spike with a tsk-tsk. "You should have someone out there."

"I did," Spike said. "I'm surrounded by idiots. What's new with you?"

"Everything." Angelus tightened his hold on the boy struggling under his arm.

"Come up against the Slayer yet?" Spike asked.

"She's cute," Angelus said. "Not too bright, though. Gave her the puppy-dog, 'I'm all tortured' act. Keeps her off my back when I'm trying to feed."

Spike laughed. "People still fall for that Anne Rice routine? What a world."

"I knew you were lying," the boy said. "Undead liar guy."

Angelus grabbed the boy's hair and pulled his collar back to expose his neck. "Wanna bite before we kill her? Hmm?"

Something isn't right, Spike thought as he stared into Angelus's eyes. "Haven't seen you in the killing fields for an age."

Since China, to be exact.

Beijing
1900

Killing the Slayer incited Spike's hunger for more than blood. He took Dru on the temple floor, heedless of the flames, serenaded by screams, aroused by the tang of the dead girl's drying blood in the air. Though they were twined in reckless ardor when the walls crumpled, they scrambled clear. Smeared with soot and reeking of smoke, they were flush with the glory of his deeds and their epic passion.

"My lit'le Spike just killed himself a slayer," Drusilla

bragged when she and Spike caught up with Darla and Angelus.

"Did you hear that?" Darla glanced at Angelus.

"Congratulations," Angelus said, looking none too pleased to hear the news. "I guess that makes you one of us."

Angelus's lack of enthusiasm didn't surprise Spike. Being outdone by Drusilla's impulsive play-mate had to hurt. The Slayer kill threw the whole bloody pecking order into turmoil. Even Darla was vis-ibly subdued. He was no longer a nuisance she had to tolerate for Dru's sake. That made it easier for him to be magnanimous, especially since Angelus was only barely back in Darla's favor.

"Don't look so glum, mate," Spike said sincerely. "Way you tell it, one slayer snuffs, another one rises. I figure there's a new Chosen One getting all Chosen as we speak."

Angelus couldn't even look him in the eye.

"I'll tell you what," Spike went on. "When and if this new bird shows up, I'll give you first crack at her."

Dru scowled, drawn to an alley. "I smell fear."

"This whole place reeks of it," Angelus said.

"It's intoxicating." Dru's body sagged as Spike came up behind her. He steadied her with both hands, until she laughed and pulled away from him.

"Let's get out of here." Angelus turned away. "This rebellion is starting to bore me."

Spike wasn't bored. He was worried. Several times in the past few months Dru had suffered swoon-ing spells for no apparent reason. He wasn't certain, but he thought they were happening more often.

Drusilla walked beside him now, a lioness playing peasant in her red tunic and flowing pants. He cast her a jaunty grin and winked. Her gaze smoldered with a desire that never seemed to wane. Then she faltered.

Spike had Dru in his arms before she fell. Lifting her up, he kissed her and carried her through the war-torn city.

When they reached the hotel, Dru insisted on being put down to walk back to their room. Since her reality wasn't always grounded in fact, Spike wasn't sure she knew the extent of her mysterious condition. He certainly didn't want Darla to suspect anything. Angelus had the soft spot of a sire for Dru, but Darla loathed weakness of any kind. Predators weeded out the old and the sick, but he would not sacrifice Dru to the primal needs of the pack.

Relieved when the other couple left to be alone, Spike hurried Dru back to their rooms. She fell into a deep slumber before dawn and slept peacefully through the battles raging outside. Despite the night's exertions, he dozed fitfully and rose often to check on her. When she awoke feeling faint and too tired to go out, he knew his mounting concern was not without merit. She had never languished like this before.

"It's just a silly case of the vapors, Spike." Propped on a lounge with pillows and a shawl, Dru smiled to assure him. "Ladies have always feigned such ailments so gentlemen will worry and wait on their every whim."

Spike smiled too, but only to hide how deeply

troubled he felt. "I'll worry and wait on you forever, Dru. You don't have to pretend to be sick."

"Please, play the game," Dru cajoled. "Surprise me with something special. I like surprises, lit'le ones with ten toes and rosy cheeks."

"I'll see what I can find," Spike promised.

Before leaving the hotel, Spike went to Darla's rooms. He didn't want her or Angelus to find Dru feeling poorly and abed. If he mentioned that Dru was in a playful mood, they would avoid her rather than risk being drawn into one of her insane scenarios.

Except Angelus was gone.

"He left?" Spike glanced at the empty white bassinet and the broken window. The lace linens were rife with the sweet smell of an infant. "Didn't want to share the morsel, did he?"

"His palate is not nearly so refined these days." Looking splendid in a green Chinese gown with gold brocade trim, Darla turned from the window. Her eyes flashed with bitter contempt. "Murderers, rapists, thieves, and scoundrels are more to his taste. He won't starve."

"When do you expect him back?" Spike asked, treading cautiously. The last time Angelus and Darla had argued, Angelus disappeared for two years. During that time, although Darla had frequently gone off on her own for food and entertainment, she had traveled and roomed with him and Dru. Now, however, Dru's occasional condition seemed to be slowly worsening. Without Angelus to keep Darla occupied, he would not be able to hide Dru's poor health indefinitely.

Spike could—and would—kill Darla to protect Dru if necessary. He didn't want to.

"Come back? Never," Darla snapped. "I won't be made a fool."

At a loss for words, Spike offered the only consolation he could think of. "Dru had a craving for children tonight. Would you like me to pick one up for you?"

"I've been betrayed, not de-fanged," Darla spat. "Besides, I can't stand the sight of you, either. Fawning all over Dru like a fatuous puppy. Get out."

Stunned by the disdain in her glowering eyes, Spike stood frozen in place. No one had spoken to him in that tone since Cecily's party the night he was changed. No one would ever speak to him that way again and live.

"Get out!" Darla screamed. "Get out now!"

No one except Darla. Spike couldn't subject himself to her vicious venom. He left to arrange transportation out of China for him and Dru.

Sunnydale
September 1997

Spike had never known Angelus to flinch at the mention of killing fields. The reaction had been subtle, but disturbing. Very disturbing.

"I'm not much for company," Angelus said.

"No, you never were." Since the Slayer was alive and well in Sunnydale, Spike asked the obvious question. "So why are you so scared of this Slayer?"

"Scared?" Angelus looked taken aback.

"Yeah," Spike answered matter-of-factly. "Time was, you would have taken her out in a heartbeat. Now look at you. I mean, this . . . tortured thing is an act, right? You're not"—he wrinkled his nose—"housebroken?"

"I saw her kill the Master," Angelus said.

Uh-huh, Spike thought. That would be the same Master whose underground abode, habits, fealty to the old ones, and prophecy Angelus had insolently insulted shortly after his making. At least that was the story Darla liked to tell. Angelus hadn't been afraid of the ancient vampire then. Of course, a lot had changed since 1760.

Spike stared into Angelus's eyes. They were the yellow eyes of a vampire, but not of a soulless demon.

"Hey," Angelus went on, "you think you can take her alone? Be my guest. I'll just feed and run." With a snarl, Angelus prepared to tap a vein in the tall boy's neck.

"Oh, don't be silly," Spike said, holding up a staying hand. He didn't want to believe the despicable truth about Angelus, but the glimmer of the spark was unmistakable. It explained a lot that had puzzled him for years. Darla hadn't chased Spike off with contemptuous insults because she thought he was a soddin' puppy. She ran him off because he was a cruel, vicious vampire—everything Angelus had been, and was no more.

"We're old friends," Spike continued. "We'll do it together. Let's drink to it."

Calling the bluff, Spike lowered his mouth toward the boy's inviting neck. Angelus moved way too slowly for a vampire needing a blood brew. Spike drew his fist back and hit the older vampire hard, sending him stumbling backward.

"You think you can fool me?" Spike bellowed. He started to walk away, but the offense was too vile. He spun around. "You were my grandsire, man! You were my . . . Yoda!"

"Things change," Angelus said calmly, as though they were having a casual disagreement over a pint.

"Not us," Spike countered. "Not demons."

The sight of the boy cowering behind Angelus for protection fed Spike's fury. Angelus, the once proud Scourge of Europe, had begun his reign of terror by killing his family and everyone in his village. Now he was one of the Slayer's groupies.

"Man, I can't believe this. You Uncle Tom!" *Enough talking,* Spike thought as he picked up the table strut he had dropped. "Come on, people. This isn't a spectator sport!"

The boy pushed open the cafeteria doors and ducked through with Angelus close behind.

Spike gripped the metal bar, intent on destroying the Angelus abomination. A vampire with a soul was more than a personal affront. It upset the balance of good and evil, and things had to be put right. However, as his snarling minions ran past to give chase, he caught an enticing scent.

Slayer. Spike paused. *Much more important than a sniveling ex-evil thing with delusions of redemption.*

"Fee, fi, fo, fum. I smell the blood of a nice, ripe" —Spike turned slowly—"girl."

The Slayer stood across the corridor, watching him. She had shed her blue sweater and carried the fire axe he had given Jack. It wasn't likely Spike would be seeing the dull boy in blue plaid again.

"Do we really need weapons for this?" Buffy asked. The touch of impertinence in her voice was sugar on the treat.

"I just like them." Smiling, Spike ran his hand across his chest. "They make me feel all manly."

Suddenly serious, he threw the metal bar down and walked toward her. The girl dropped the axe and stood her ground, but her confidence would be easily undermined when the proper psychological pressure was applied.

"The last slayer I killed," Spike said, "she begged for her life." That wasn't exactly true. Nikki had never begged anyone for anything. She had willingly passed the Slayer torch so her son wouldn't be a target in the good-versus-evil crossfire, but Buffy didn't know that.

With her hands clasped behind her back, the Slayer moved toward him with a sassy sashay. She wasn't all aquiver with fear, but he could tell she respected him—one adversary to another. That was smart, and his assessment of her went up another notch. Still, it couldn't hurt to massage her ego. Too much confidence could be just as fatal as too little.

Spike matched her sashay with a brash strut. "You don't strike me as the begging kind."

"You shouldn't have come here," Buffy said softly.

"No, I messed up your doilies and stuff, but I just got so bored." When she didn't react, Spike added a bold helping of bravado. "I'll tell you what. As a personal favor from me to you, I'll make it quick. It won't hurt a bit."

"No, Spike, it's going to hurt a lot."

You've got that right, Spike thought as he threw the first punch.

The Slayer ducked under his arm, countered a second swing, missed with a kick, and landed one on Spike's jaw. Employing a mix of martial arts and basic street brawling, Spike gave as good as he got, biding his time until he caught her in the stomach and heaved her into the wall. The Slayer scrambled to her feet, but not quickly enough to avoid another blow.

She was good, Spike realized. Less disciplined than China Doll and not as reliant on brute force as Nikki, but Buffy had something else—a secret Slayer ingredient. Whatever it was, it was giving him a fight worth showing up for.

Invigorated by a volley of slayer punches to the torso, Spike grabbed on and flung her into another wall. He drew his arm back to flatten her pretty face, but she stepped clear and his fist smashed through the wall. Stuck for a moment, he couldn't evade a kick in the back.

"Now, that hurt." Enraged, Spike grabbed a two-by-four stud in the wall and pulled a section free. He slammed the Slayer with the board as he turned, knocking her down. "But not as much as this will."

Spike knew the fight was over except for the actual death part. The girl was down with the wind knocked out of her. She wouldn't stay down long, but he only needed a second to finish her off. He raised the two-by-four to strike the killing blow—and hesitated when he looked into Buffy's eyes.

She wasn't sad or reconciled to defeat or tired of it

all or ready to quit. This Slayer had a mega-dose of defiance and a determined will to live—and win. She might lose, but she wouldn't give up.

Good for you, Spike thought as he tightened his grip, *but it won't save you.* He was so focused on the girl that he didn't sense someone else coming up behind him. He fell when something hard and sharp hit him in the head. Stunned, he rolled onto his back and stared up into the furious face of the woman Buffy had rushed out of the cafeteria. She had clobbered him with the infernal axe!

"You get the hell away from my daughter."

The Slayer's mum wasn't kidding around. Spike could move ten times as fast, and he was a hundred times stronger, but he never underestimated the power of a mother to protect her young. Besides, the Slayer was back on her feet again, shaken but ready to go at it. He wanted to fight the girl, but not when she was worried about keeping her mother alive. It had to be a fair fight to count for anything.

"Women!" Furious, Spike pushed the broken stud off, jumped up and back out the window, and ran.

Sunnydale
September 2002

"Still running too, aren't you, Spike?" *Angelus* said. "From all your lies."

Angelus knew too much, and Spike didn't want to talk to him. He watched the Slayer try to slam the storeroom door closed, but zombie-man was still in the way.

"'Once he starts something, he doesn't stop until everything in his path is dead.' Yeah, right." *Angelus* rolled his eyes. "I actually told the Slayer that when you first came to Sunnydale, Spike. I probably should have qualified it, though. Everything in your path dead— except the Slayer."

Don't listen. Door's closing. Spike stared as the metal door cleared the cranky spirit and clunked closed. Buffy quickly threw the latch over and locked the dead bolt.

"You could have killed her on Parent-Teacher Night, ended it all right there," *Angelus* went on, "but you didn't. Why not?"

"They'll probably show up in a sec." Buffy backed away from the door.

"Nobody comes in here," Spike said. It was okay to talk to Buffy. She thought she knew things, but she didn't know everything. "It's just the three of us."

"Spike, have you seen Dawn?" Buffy asked. "She came down here with some kids—"

"You just don't get it, Spike." *Angelus* cast a lecherous glance at Buffy.

But It wasn't Angelus. It was something else, a powerful, primal evil that knew everything. The Other knew he had gotten his soul restored—deliberately. That's why It sent the dead people, to punish him, to make sure he knew that a quest for salvation was futile. Evil hated to lose.

"You're a coward, Spike." *Angelus* snorted with derision. "You won't even face the truth of your own miserable existence."

"Don't you think I'm trying?" Spike blurted out, squeezing his eyes shut.

The girl watched him closely. Not like that time in the cafeteria when she wanted to put a stake in his heart. More like she was worried—no, she wouldn't worry about him. It was like she was scared. And she should be, locked in a storeroom with a crazy man. Not to mention three manifest spirits that wanted to hurt her and a very Big Bad under the ground that wanted to hurt everyone.

"Once evil, always evil," *Angelus* said. "There's nothing you can do to atone for the horrors of your past and no way you can escape history's hold."

"I'm not fast. Not a quick study." Spike opened his eyes and looked past Buffy at *Angelus*. He had tried so hard to rise above the ridicule, to forget the torments of childhood that had driven his agenda as a vampire. But they festered down deep and couldn't be ripped out.

"I dropped my board in the water and the chalk all ran." Spike's voice was choked with tears. The schoolmaster had had no patience with clumsy children. "Sure to be caned." He laughed. "Should have seen that coming."

"You should have killed the Slayer," *Angelus* persisted. "Think of all the trouble you could have saved yourself."

Too late now. When Spike saw Buffy coming closer, her gaze riveted on his chest, he pulled the edges of his shirt closed. He looked away and moved into the corner, but the girl kept coming. She always kept coming. To kill him or scold him, ask a favor—always there, but not there.

Buffy's eyes filled with pity when she saw the red slashes. "What did you do?"

"I tried to—I tried to cut it out." He looked away. He wanted to be free of everything that hurt—the chip, the spark, his heart . . .

"Wouldn't do any good to cut out a dead heart," *Dru* said. "But it's worse than dead, isn't it, Spike? It's nothing but ashes now."

Buffy's cell phone rang, and she turned away to answer.

Dru circled the Slayer like a jungle cat, waiting for the right moment to pounce. She smiled as she sang, "Ring around the rosy, pocket full of posies, ashes, ashes, we all fall down. . . ."

Sunnydale
September 1997

Spike walked the streets of Sunnydale after he left the high school, grabbing a quick meal behind a minimart, learning his way about town, and trying to wrap his mind around being outmaneuvered by a middle-aged mother with an axe. The only thing good about the whole sorry episode was that nobody had seen it, except the Slayer.

But that's the only good thing, Spike thought as he walked across the factory parking lot with the first rays of dawn nipping at his heels. The surviving underlings had probably hightailed it straight back to the brick building to tell wonder boy all about Spike's spectacular failure. He looked up at the grime-covered windows, wondering how bad things were for him inside. It was a lousy way to end the night.

Dru was waiting to comfort him when he arrived. "Spike, did she hurt you?"

"It was close, baby, but—"

"Aw, come here." Drusilla pulled his head onto her shoulder and stroked his neck.

"A slayer with family and friends," Spike said, disgusted. "That sure as hell wasn't in the brochure."

"You'll kill her," Dru said with absolute conviction. "And then we'll have a nice celebration."

"Yeah, a party." Spike looked toward the stairs. The Anointed One sat on his metal tub conferring with Goatee. That treacherous goon hadn't lost any time staking his claim as the little creep's favorite.

"Yeah," Dru murmured wistfully, "with streamers and songs."

Black streamers and dirges and gagged baby dolls all in a row, Spike thought. Dru loved macabre parties, and he hated to disappoint her.

"How's the Annoying One?" Spike asked.

"He doesn't want to play." Dru seemed put out.

"It figures." Spike was not looking forward to the obligatory debasement. "Well, I guess I'd better go make nice."

Smiling through gritted teeth, Spike walked over and knelt on one knee before the boy.

"You failed," the Anointed One stated flatly.

No kidding, Spike thought.

"I, um . . . offer penance." Spike cringed inwardly. He hadn't really said that, had he?

"Penance?" Goatee sputtered with indignation. "You should lay down your life. Our numbers are depleted . . ."

No loss there.

Goatee ended his outburst with a flourish. "The Feast of St. Vigeous has been ruined by your impatience!"

"I was rash," Spike said stiffly. "And if I had it to do all over again—"

There was only one thing Spike hated more than losing a fight, which almost never happened, and that was groveling—which had never happened until now. He couldn't change the fact that he had indulged his curiosity and waited a few seconds too long to take out the Slayer, but he sure as hell didn't have to kowtow to a brat with an inflated sense of his own importance and power.

"Who am I kidding?" Spike laughed as he rose to his feet. Bearing the brunt of unjustified disgrace brought out the worst in his usually charming nature. "I would do it exactly the same—only I'd do this first!"

"No!" The boy cried out as Spike hoisted him onto his shoulder.

With a firm grip on the Master's insufferable choice, Spike strode to the center of the room, repelling Goatee with a boot to the chest. He pulled open the door of the barred cage and dumped the squirming boy inside. There was only one reason for the cage to be there in the first place. The little guy liked to fry vampires.

Showtime! Spike locked the door, turned to the pulley assembly on a nearby post, and hauled on the chains to hoist the cage to the roof.

"From now on," Spike announced loudly, "we're going to have a little less ritual and a little more fun around here." He pulled on another chain, opening the skylight.

The boy shrieked in agony as the morning sun turned him into cinders. Spike paused for a split second's reflection. The Anointed One had had a short, thoroughly unremarkable reign, barely worth the ink to pen a mention in the histories being written.

Except that I toasted the little bugger, Spike thought with a satisfied grin at Dru. She looked thrilled, which more than made up for his brief brush with humility. He took her hand. "Let's see what's on TV."

Dru lagged a bit on the way to their corner of the factory. Spike didn't rush her, knowing that the journey from New Orleans, the stress of settling into a new place, and the anxious anticipation of dealing with a slayer had taken a toll.

"You'll have to eat something tonight, kitten." Spike switched the TV on to a morning news show. The incidents of murder and mayhem committed by humans on a daily basis were always entertaining.

"I would have tea and scones with the lit'le people, but I'm feeling a bit out of sorts." Dru lifted a large doll in a green gown, dropped it, and stamped it repeatedly with her foot. "That will teach Miss Martha to laugh at her elders."

"Did someone laugh at you?" Spike asked as he moved to her side. He wouldn't want to be the vampire that had hurt Dru's feelings.

"He didn't care for my clothes." Dru pursed her

lips. "Asked what self-respecting vampire would wear a pretty white dress."

"Who did?" Spike tensed, his anger mounting. "I'll cut out his tongue and stuff it down his throat before I kill him."

"You can't." Dru smiled. "The wretched lit'le thing took a bad turn in the sun this morning. Perhaps, I should burn my dress—"

"I love your dress," Spike assured her. She swayed as he slipped his arm around her waist. "Would you like to lie down?"

"Not just now." Dru picked up Miss Martha and set the doll back on the shelf. "No more laughing or you'll be ashes by tomorrow."

Weary from the long night and still furious about losing the opening round with the Slayer, Spike took off his duster. He hung the coat on a bracket that clamped a pipe to the wall, then sank into a chair by the TV and propped up his feet. He couldn't hear the newscaster's account of a deadly fire over Dru's singing, but he had too much on his mind to care.

"Ring around the rosy, pocket full of posies, ashes, ashes, all fall down—"

Spike had learned to tune out the fourteenth-century children's song about the bubonic plague. The images seemed innocent until one realized that the plague victims' skin had turned rose red, and the living had used flowers—posies—to mask the odor of burning bodies. The ditty about death was one of Dru's favorites.

"Don't interrupt me when I'm singing." Dru dropped

the large doll again. "If we were having a party, Miss Martha, you wouldn't be able to come."

Spike swore under his breath. He hated making Dru unhappy and vowed to hold a bash with all the pomp, ceremony, and bloody games her black heart desired as soon as he killed the Slayer.

Tiring of her plastic and porcelain entourage, Dru kissed Spike's cheek. "I will lie down a bit now. I'm feeling a lit'le faint."

Spike helped Dru into bed, covered her with a quilt, and returned to his chair. Lowering the volume on the TV, he gave himself over to his thoughts. Killing the Slayer was on his to do list, but now that the Master's brat was gone, he could take care of her on his schedule. He wouldn't have anything to celebrate if Dru became too weak to sustain her undead body. Unless he found a cure, she would suffer horribly for years, growing weaker and thinner until she dried up and crumbled into nothing.

Spike would not let that happen.

He had scoured the occult libraries, interrogated the masterminds of the medicinal black arts, and followed every lead to find a charm, potion, or spell to cure Dru's malady. Her wasting condition was rare, but not unknown among vampires and those that revered or served them. The research trail had led him to Josephus du Lac, a theologian and mathematician who had been excommunicated at the turn of the century. He had belonged to a sect that created unusual rituals and spells for the evil. The *du Lac Manuscript*, a handwritten text bound in embossed leather, reportedly contained the ritual to restore a sick and weak vampire to health.

But no one knew where the book was.

The *du Lac Manuscript* had vanished from a university library in Poland when Hitler invaded in 1939. It had surfaced again in the 1950s and was acquired by a New England museum for an extensive exhibit about witchcraft and the dark disciplines. The lack of operating funds had forced the exhibit to close, and the book had been sold to a museum patron and collector. A year ago, in 1996 when the dead collector's estate was being settled, the volume came up missing. A search was not undertaken, since the rich old duffer had made a habit of giving his possessions to whoever admired them. Spike had taken Dru to New Orleans based on a rumor that the book would be offered in a private sale. The rumor was false, and the trail had grown cold again.

Spike wasn't about to give up. Once he set his mind to doing something, he did it. The *du Lac Manuscript* was out there, and his priority was to find it before Dru sickened beyond hope. He was no less intent on killing the Slayer, but she had a temporary reprieve.

Unfortunately, so did Angelus. Spike had crossed paths with his old mentor since China, but not under circumstances that had revealed Angelus's foul conversion. How could it have happened to one of the most vicious, unscrupulous vampires in the world? By what means could a vampire regain his soul? Fascinated—and not a little revolted—Spike had to have answers to his questions. Having the feeble spark of his own soul find its way home was a fate he wanted to avoid at all costs.

"Ashes sprinkled on the cakes . . . ," Dru muttered in her sleep.

Spike smiled at the frail creature he loved so deeply. He would always be grateful to Angelus for making Drusilla, but it was hard to believe he was once desperate to win Angelus's respect.

Sunnydale
September 2002

Spike sat on the floor, holding his head in his hand and muttering gibberish. His persona had been peeled away and his emotions bared in front of Buffy. The exposure was more than he could handle. Everything he had been was gone—stirred and dissolved in pain, guilt, and self-loathing.

"Nobody ever respected you, William." *Cecily* stood over him, grinding him into the dirt with her haughty bearing.

"Where are you?" Buffy asked into the phone.

"You were the parlor jester," *Cecily* went on, "invited to our soirees as a source of amusement."

"That's why I liked him," *Dru* said. "He was so good at making up little games."

Buffy was still talking to Dawn. "Yeah, they came after me, too."

"I especially liked hunt-and-kill-the-Slayer! The danger was intoxicating before she made you all soft and squishy." *Dru* curled her hands into claws and struck at Buffy with a menacing hiss. But unlike the grungy spirit people, the Other had no substance and couldn't do any physical harm.

"So far, to piss me off," Buffy said into the small phone.

Dru was angry too. Spike hugged the corner, wishing she'd leave, knowing she wouldn't.

"Yes, I am quite upset." *Dru* leaned over, glaring at him. "You were it, Spike, but you didn't tag the Slayer. You broke the rules and let her get away."

"Oh, I'm damage-bound." Buffy sounded just a tad frazzled. "I just can't figure them. Ghosts can't touch you, and zombies can't disappear, so I don't know what we're dealing with—"

Spike hacked through his tangled thoughts, ignoring *Dru* to make a clear space. "Not ghosts."

"Hold on." Buffy slapped her hand over the phone and turned to him. "You know what they are?"

The voices suddenly clambered to be heard, speaking one after another, trying to confuse him so he couldn't help the girl. Spike pushed them back.

"Manifest spirits, controlled by a talisman and raised to seek vengeance," he explained. "A four-year-old could figure it."

"Don't get cocky," *Angelus* admonished him. "You haven't figured your way out of this, and this is going to do much worse than kill you. You'll be trapped by your own madness and despair."

Chapter Five

"I don't want to be here alone," Dru said. "Miss Edith won't speak to me anymore."

"Maybe that's because she has a gag over her mouth," Spike said, putting on his duster. He rarely lost patience with Drusilla, but she had an uncanny habit of pestering him when he was pressed about something important.

"I haven't been to the park to hunt in ever so long," Dru whined. "I miss sinking my teeth into someone whose blood is hot from running."

"Is that the problem, then?" Spike's tone was heavy with sarcasm. "Tell you what, pet. I'll fetch someone back and chase the bloke around a few minutes before you eat. Heat and serve."

Dru's lower lip began to quiver.

"Oh, don't cry." Spike wilted under Dru's injured gaze. Catering to her delicate constitution and whims was time-consuming and often exasperating, but he rarely complained and despised himself when he did. She had rescued him from an abyss of despair when she changed him, a debt he could never fully repay. Curing her affliction would add some credits to his side of the ledger, though, and tonight he had a lead on the *du Lac Manuscript*.

"It's not that I don't want your company," Spike said, "but I have business to take care of before I get groceries. You'd be bored, believe me."

"I'm bored here." Dru frowned.

"And weak," Spike reminded her.

Dru had no interest in books or the tedious task of tracking a missing one down, not even if it held the secret to restoring her to eternal life. He had to concentrate on his quest, not attend to her ills and snits. She couldn't come.

But Dru was in a stubborn mood. "I'm strong enough to prey on the feeble ones, the very young and very old."

"Look, I'll take you out for homeless people tomorrow night," Spike said. "The benches around town are a smorgasbord of derelicts. In the meantime, why not amuse yourself with our resident gang of fools?"

"We could play a game," Dru said, brightening. "Can you think of one? You're so clever at making up games."

Before Spike could answer, Hank and Lucius rushed over in furious vamp mode. Spike had defended his right to rule several times since flash frying the Anointed One. Goatee had been the first to fall in a failed ambush attempt. Although neither Hank nor Lucius had challenged him, they both wanted to be his second-in-command. He didn't really need a lieutenant, but playing them off each other had been entertaining.

"What's the problem?" Spike asked.

"Hank won't take his turn on watch." Lucius folded his arms and glared at the smaller male.

Hank glared back. "I'm hungry."

"Why didn't you get something to eat last night, when you weren't on duty?" Spike struggled to hide his irritation.

"I did," Hank said. "I'm still hungry."

"He's always hungry," Lucius shot back.

Spike was no longer entertained. "Lucius, what would you say if I ordered you to take Hank's watch?"

Lucius didn't hesitate. "You're the boss."

"Yes, and I'm going out." Spike turned a chilling smile on Hank. "From now on, Lucius will be the boss when I'm gone, of everyone except Dru."

"Yes!" Lucius yanked air with his fist.

"You'll keep Dru happy, of course." Spike cocked an eyebrow at Lucius, but there was no question the vampire would do anything to stay in her good graces. "And Dru will tell me if anyone gives you a hard time. Now, get out of here."

Spike rolled his eyes as the two vampires raced

away. Since he had established his supremacy, he had spent way too much time settling petty squabbles among the troops. He had won their respect and guaranteed Dru's safety, but they hadn't paid dearly enough for the inconvenience and hassle.

"Have a scavenger hunt, Dru," Spike suggested. "Send everyone out for prey that won't be easy to find."

"Like a butterfly collection." Dru paused, thinking. "I could ask for a bald man with bad teeth and a beer belly."

"There you go." Spike leaned toward her, beaming. "Twins might be interesting, or a midget with curly hair and a dimple. And just in case you want to keep them for a while, I'll pick up dinner at The Bronze on my way home."

Spike kissed her on the cheek and left before she found fault with his game or another reason to delay him.

Unlike many denizens of the underworld set, Spike wasn't a purist. He didn't believe using mundane modern methods to achieve his evil ends betrayed his supernatural heritage. The Yellow Pages and a telephone had uncovered a used bookstore called A Rare Read. The proprietor specialized in finding and obtaining obscure volumes.

Spike entered the store through a side door. There were no customers, but a bearded man wearing a *Star Trek* T-shirt sat behind a cluttered checkout counter staring at a computer monitor. Except for electric lights and a phone, the computer was the only modern device in the place.

"I close in twenty minutes," the man said without looking up. "Browse fast."

"I doubt you have the book I want on the premises," Spike said, taking in the details of the store at a glance.

The walkways between the stacks, tables, and shelves were clear, but every other square foot of space was stuffed with books: new and old, large and small, fat and thin, leather bound and paperback. A pair of bookcases with glass doors blocked the front window. A permanent haze of dust hung in the air and coated the shelves, apparently impervious to drafts, feather dusters, and furniture polish. A Rare Read had been in business for a very long time, longer than the rude man at the computer was old.

"Are you Sidney Cranston?" Spike asked, stepping up to the counter. *If not, I'm going to kill you because you're obnoxious.*

"The Third, but I'm the only Sidney Cranston that matters." The man glanced up. "The other two are dead."

"There's a lot of that going around," Spike quipped. Sidney Cranston the Third did not in any way resemble the literary types he had met before. He was no more than thirty, with shaggy brown hair, John Lennon wire-rimmed glasses, and a rose-twined-anchor tattoo on his forearm.

"Tell me about it." Sidney swiveled his stool to face front. "Sunnydale's the epicenter of death from weird but unknown causes."

"I'm looking for a book," Spike said.

"Most people who come here are," Sidney shot back.

Spike suspected Sidney's father had been the expert touted in the Yellow Pages advertisement, but there was no harm asking his questions. If Sidney Three didn't have the answers, he'd take the scruffy, smart-ass bookworm home as his contribution to Dru's collection.

"One-of-a-kind," Spike went on, "embossed leather binding, about a hundred years old, called the *du Lac Manuscript*."

"You're kidding." Sidney looked incredulous. "I saw something about that text a couple weeks ago."

"You're kidding. Where is it?"

"Tell you in a minute." The young man turned back to the computer and tapped a few keys. "I've got the most comprehensive database on rare and unusual books in town, except for maybe Professor Dalton. I update every day."

Spike waited, trying not to appear too impatient. If Sidney had a bead on the *du Lac Manuscript*, Spike would probably let him live. There was no telling when he might need to locate another rare text.

"Here we go," Sidney said. "Roman Shaw bought it at a private sale in Orleans, Massachusetts a month ago."

Spike blinked. "There's an Orleans without "New" in front of it?"

"On Cape Cod," Sidney said. "Right above the elbow. Never been there myself."

Spike threw up his hands. "What is it with rumors that people can't get their facts straight?"

"Beats me." Sidney shrugged.

"So where do I find this Roman bloke that's got my book?"

"Mr. Shaw probably doesn't have the book." Sidney closed the window on the monitor. "He's an agent. He buys rare books and artifacts for clients who don't have the time to track things down themselves."

"All right, then." Spike nodded at the phone sitting on a stack of old *Atlantic Monthly* magazines. "Ring him up and ask who has it now."

"Wouldn't do any good," Sidney said. "Roman Shaw doesn't talk about his clients or their business transactions, not to me, anyway."

He'll talk to me, Spike thought.

Sidney frowned. "But he might tell Professor Dalton, especially if this *du Lac Manuscript* was a coup. They've been friends for years."

"A professor at UC Sunnydale?" Spike asked.

"Crestwood College," Sidney said. "He teaches ancient languages."

"You've been right helpful, Sidney the Third." Spike smiled. "I'll be back."

Spike decided to put off paying a visit to the professor. Dru's behavior could be erratic when she was bored or upset, and she had been both tonight. And, on further reflection, he realized his impromptu game could backfire. The minions might object to letting Dru "collect" their prey when they had worked harder than usual to get it. He didn't want to be away from the factory longer than necessary, and he headed straight for The Bronze.

Sunnydale
September 2002

The instant Spike finished telling Buffy about manifest spirits, she turned away.

"Hang tight," Buffy told Dawn, speaking into her cell phone. "I'll find you. These things can hurt you. You can hurt them, too. Find a weapon. I'll come for you."

Glory appeared behind Buffy. Her red dress reminded Spike of blood, and hurt his eyes.

"Spike, you gonna help me out?" Buffy asked, shoving the cell phone into her back pocket.

"Why help her?" *Glory* asked. "She never appreciates it."

Yes, she does, Spike thought. The Slayer was suddenly frozen in place, but his mind raced, as though he had been isolated from real time.

"Oh, right." *Glory* uttered a short, derisive laugh. "You let a god pound your pretty-boy face to protect the key, but did Buffy care? Not even a little."

Lie! Spike wanted to shout in protest, but his mouth wouldn't move. Even so, he knew *Glory* was wrong. Buffy had cared. She had.

"You don't know that. You *can't* know that." *Glory* got in his face, smiling, determined to warp his perceptions. "You're insane."

Spike flipped through his memories, looking for the truth that would expose *Glory's* lie.

"I practically turned you into mincemeat!" *Glory* exclaimed. "But all Buffy cared about was her precious kid sister."

Yes, the Niblet. Spike latched onto an image of Dawn. That's why the Slayer was in the basement now. She was looking for Dawn.

"And as soon as Dawnie is safe, Buffy will forget about you," *Glory* taunted, "just as she did a moment ago and just as she did back then."

No, that wasn't how it went. Spike stared at the Slayer. The Other didn't want him to remember, but he had to remember. It was important.

"You want those memories back?" *Glory* asked. "Fine. Remember how Buffy treated you like dirt. She didn't trust you, couldn't trust you, wouldn't trust you—about anything."

Except Dawn, Spike realized, fighting the Other's influence. Buffy had once posed as the Buffy-bot and come to see him in the crypt. She had studied his cuts and bruises, wanting to know if he had betrayed Dawn to Glory.

I didn't tell. I wouldn't do anything to hurt Little-bit. Spike had been desperate to make Buffy understand, was still desperate. She had believed him, kissed him, told him that what he had done was real and that she wouldn't forget.

"Big deal." *Glory* grinned. "The Slayer couldn't remember anything after she dove off my tower."

The Other replayed that memory, forcing Spike to watch as Buffy fell from the sky onto the pavement and died.

No! Stricken, Spike retreated from the unbearable pain, unwilling to experience it again. He let himself sink deeper into the mire of twisted thought where reality didn't matter. The Other took over and began spouting nonsense to Buffy about the Hellmouth.

"This is my home," the Other said in Spike's voice. "I belong here, always been here."

As he descended into the well of sorrow, Spike looked through the Other into Buffy's eyes. He saw something . . . not sure what. Pity? Regret? No—whatever it was, it stopped his plunge into the mental maelstrom and helped him shake off the Other for a moment.

"Cheers for stopping by," Spike said, turning his back. He couldn't face the Slayer, but he couldn't let her leave without an explanation. "It's in the walls."

Buffy paused.

"The Slayer's still there," *Dru* said. "Floating all around you, but never, never yours. Poor lit'le Spike."

Harmony rolled her eyes. "Slayer this and Slayer that. She's everywhere, haunting him, just like he said. It'll never end."

No, the pain will never end, Spike thought. He clutched at the wall, unable to still the whimpers in his throat. It just burned and burned, a spark cast into the eternal fires of hell. No one ever told that secret—that hell was inside.

"I'll get back to you." Buffy unlatched the door, kicked it open, and left.

"All this pain and angst didn't have to happen, Spike," *Angelus* said. "You always were too impulsive for your own good. Killing without thinking, never getting the maximum bang for your bite."

Spike hung his head. His mentor had been an artist,

creating and compounding misery. Angelus had reveled in making his victims suffer before he killed them—or turned them. He had made Drusilla insane, killing her family, driving her into a convent, and changing her on the day she took her Holy Orders. Nothing less than diabolically brilliant, Spike conceded.

Angelus plotted and planned. Spike had been more of a spur-of-the-moment, whatever-works-now killer.

"All you had to do was pick a friend and kill it," *Angelus* said. "Then the Slayer would have been drowning in guilt and remorse when you fought her. How hard was that?"

Harder than Spike ever imagined.

Sunnydale
October 1997

Sunny D. is just full of surprises, Spike thought as he slipped into The Bronze, *some pleasant and some not so pleasant.* The warehouse club was holding some kind of masquerade with an international theme, a decidedly pleasant turn of events. He scanned with a critical eye the wide selection of Grade-A-prime teens decked out in costumes. The cuisine was All-American. He just had to choose which exotic package Dru would like best.

Spanish lady or Cossack? Spike glanced at the couple standing on the far side of the entrance.

Between tracking down the *du Lac Manuscript,* expanding his and Dru's personal space in the factory, and managing the subordinates, Spike had not had a lot of R & R lately. Rather than grab the first succulent bit that caught his eye, he hung back in the shadows to watch the floor show and choose an entrée at his leisure.

A local band called Dingoes Ate My Baby was pounding out a baleful tune with a beat. The drummer and lead guitarist had their acts together, but half the lead singer's words were unintelligible.

"She's in ecstasy," the boy sang. ". . . falls down heavenly, fake's desire . . ."

"Amateurs," Spike muttered as a tall brunette walked through the entrance. She wore a flower in her hair that matched a lei around her neck. The pink blossoms complemented a two-piece blue and white Hawaiian outfit.

"Hey, Cordelia," the bouncer greeted the girl. "You look terrific."

"Thanks, Boomer." Cordelia flashed him a dazzling smile as she entered the club.

Spike appraised Cordelia as potential fodder. She had dressed to get attention and, judging by the adolescent eyes that turned her way, she had succeeded.

"Ooh! Near faux pas." The tropical femme fatale sharpened her claws on a meek girl in Eskimo fur. "I almost wore the same thing."

Take no prisoners, Spike thought as Cordelia breezed by her target. Then he realized that the girl in the parka was the Slayer's pal Red. Reeking of tantalizing innocence, she would be an interesting addition to Dru's collection. The harpoon was a nice touch, but he didn't want anything mucking up the cure for Dru. A slayer out to avenge a friend's death would be a major complication. He tracked the Hawaiian charmer instead.

"Hey, where's Sven?" a girl dressed as a geisha asked.

"I keep trying to ditch him," Cordelia said. "He's like one of those dogs you leave at the Grand Canyon on vacation. It follows you back across four states."

Ouch, Spike thought. Cordelia's friends laughed, but the big boy in the Viking suit had his leather knickers in a bunch at the insult.

"See?" Cordelia said when Sven walked up. "My own speechless boomerang."

"He's kinda cute," the geisha observed. "Maybe it's nice skipping all that small talk."

"Small talk? How about simple instruction?" Cordelia turned to Sven and spoke in a tone people usually reserved for the very dense or the very deaf. "Get punchy. You. Fruit drinky."

Spike clenched his jaw. Cordelia was a sarcastic snob. She reminded him of Cecily and her circle of elite, pompous friends. He would enjoy killing the Hawaiian bimbo, except that Dru wanted *fresh,* hot blood. Cordelia, the luau lady with the acidic attitude, would be dead long before he got her back to the factory. He'd have to kill her to make her stop talking.

"He can follow me." The geisha took Sven's arm and led him off.

Sven would be big enough to sustain Dru for a couple of days. But, given the verbal abuse Cordelia had just dumped on the student Viking, it wouldn't be sporting to kill him.

"We've been born before," the singer shouted into the mike. "We'll be born again . . ."

"Devon is so cool," a girl behind Spike said. "He can sing to me all night, but he's probably dating someone."

"I think he's going out with Cordelia," another girl answered. "Or did or wants to or something."

Figures, Spike thought. Although different standards determined who was accepted into a society's top tiers, the basic rules stayed the same. The rich and popular few banded together to the exclusion of everyone else. In his day, heritage and wealth had been the foundation of social status. In an American high school, athletic prowess and beauty were the deciding factors. The system hadn't changed in the one hundred and seventeen years of Spike's existence as a vampire. It was still sick and unfair.

As Spike eased back into the crowd, the Slayer's other sidekick came in. The tall boy swaggered in a black hat and poncho with a cigar hanging unlit from his mouth, but the tough guy getup didn't negate the boy's inner nerd. The dark-haired beauty clinging to his hand completely out-classed him. Also, Spike noted with a laugh, the babe had outlived him. She was dead.

Curious, Spike moved closer as the couple did a quick stroll around the dance floor then joined Red, the Eskimo girl.

"Wow," Red said. "You guys look great."

"I love your costume." The boy's date sounded sincere. "It's very authentic."

"Thanks." Red smiled tightly.

"Yeah, you look . . . um . . ."—The boy fumbled for the right word—"snug."

"That's what I was going for," Red countered.

Like hell you were. Spike scoffed internally. It was clear Red's feelings were damaged.

"Where's Buffy?" Red turned stiffly, unable to move her arms in the heavy coat. "Weren't you and Ampata supposed to pick her up, Xander?"

"Hmm—what, Willow?" The boy—Xander—dragged his mooning gaze away from Ampata. "Did you say something?"

"Isn't Buffy coming?" Willow asked again.

"No," Xander said. "She had some stuff to do with Giles."

Spike wondered who Giles was, but didn't dwell on it. Eventually he'd find out everything he needed to know about everyone connected to the Slayer. For now, the immediate situation was loaded with suspense and was almost as compelling as the afternoon soaps. He hated to admit it, but he wanted to see what happened next.

Unlike Cordelia, who felt entitled to everyone's oxygen, Willow expected to be ignored. It was obvious she had a bad case of the longings for Xander, who was ignoring her. Xander, lacking a vampire's ability to sense such things, apparently didn't realize that his hot date was stone-cold dead.

What made me think the suburbs would be boring? Spike wondered as Willow excused herself. A short boy in an Australian bush hat sat down at the table. He stared into space, lost and alone, not even "in" with the average kids that laughed and danced around him.

Speaking of which, Xander and Ampata huddled under the metal staircase, listening to the music. *Thirty seconds,* Spike thought, *and he'll ask her to dance.*

"Take a moment," the singer warbled, "out of time, I'm standing right behind."

"Do you, um—" Xander stammered. "Would you like to, uh—you know."

"I'd love to dance," the dead date said coyly.

On the dot.

Under ordinary circumstances, Spike was good for about ten minutes of watching prey party before he singled someone out and left to eat. The only thing keeping his interest now was the unbelievable predictability of the Slayer players. The more he learned about Buffy's close cohorts, the less concerned he was that the Slayer's Scooby Gang would present any serious impediments to his plans.

Xander ditched the hat, the poncho, and the cigar and took Ampata's hand. As they walked onto the dance floor, he didn't notice Willow standing nearby, looking forlorn and forsaken. She was totally and pathetically oblivious to the lead guitar player, who couldn't take his eyes off her.

Spike turned his attention back to Xander and his partner. The boy was lost in Ampata's adoring gaze and unaware that her hand had just shriveled.

A reconstituted mummy, Spike surmised, *with a*

short shelf life. Considering how quickly and aggressively the girl's body had started to revert, she would need a life-force fix soon to retain her youthful good looks. *But it won't be Xander,* Spike realized as Ampata abruptly abandoned the boy.

Stunned, Xander hesitated before going after her, and lost Ampata in the crowd. "Okay. At least I can rule out something I said."

Spike followed Ampata. He had firsthand knowledge about many bizarre beings, but he had never seen a mummy in action and didn't want to miss a rare opportunity.

The Australian bush boy was sitting on the metal stairway, watching the dance floor he would probably never set foot on with a girl. Ampata headed straight for him.

"Is there a back door?" Ampata asked her unsuspecting life-force donor.

"Back door?" The boy's hand went limp and he almost spilled his soda.

"Yes," Ampata pleaded. "My father forbade me to come to the dance, and I think he's waiting outside. If he finds me—"

"There's an exit backstage." The boy pointed.

"Would you show me?" Ampata begged, hiding her withered hand behind her back.

"Sure." Leaving his drink, the boy hurried down the stairs and motioned for her to follow. "I'm Jonathan, in case you wanted to know."

She didn't, Spike thought as he shadowed victim and killer-seductress to a storage area in the rear of the building. He found a spot in the dark with an unobstructed view.

Jonathan was helplessly in the thrall of the beautiful girl as she removed his hat and ran her dried hand through his hair. The girl's focus narrowed to the life she needed to steal to survive.

"Your hands feel kinda . . . rough," Jonathan said. "Aren't you with Xander?"

A flicker of remorse touched Ampata's face, but it quickly passed. "Do I look like I'm with Xander?"

Spike rolled his eyes when Ampata drew Jonathan's face closer. He felt let down that her methods weren't more original. Dozens of demonic parasites used kissing to drain humans of one thing or another: information, will, or life force.

"Ampata!" Xander called out.

The sound snapped Jonathan free of the girl's mesmerizing gaze. The lucky runt grabbed his hat—"That's my cue to leave."—and ran.

Although Spike was intrigued by the new plot twist and Xander's arrival on the scene, he only wanted to spare a few minutes more. The longer he was absent from the factory, the greater the chance that chaos might erupt. The minions tended to eat on the run, not carry the prey home to play with first. If no one thought to gag the specimens, their screams might attract unwanted attention from the authorities. Lucius was the brightest of the bunch, but he was still not equipped to handle an uprising.

He should have gotten Dru her blooming bird so she wouldn't be lonely when he had to be gone. That went to the top of his to do list, along with contacting Professor Dalton.

"There you are," Xander said to Ampata, relieved to find his wayward date. "Why'd you run away?"

Spike waited to see how the scene played out, knowing that the Slayer wouldn't blame him if the mummy-girl killed Xander. Vampires didn't freeze-dry their victims.

"Because," Ampata said, looking wretched. "I do not deserve you."

"What—" Xander cut off a startled laugh as he walked toward her. "You think that you don't deserve me?" Then he did laugh. "Man, I love you."

Tears welled up in Ampata's eyes.

"Are those tears of joy?" Xander asked. "Pain? Revulsion?"

"I am very happy," Ampata confessed.

Spike suspected that was true. Primitive South American cultures had been superstitious and extraordinarily bloodthirsty. The girl had died before she was grown, probably before she had the chance to experience love. As demonic fates went, he reflected, being a vampire was preferable to just about everything else in the evil-entities catalog.

"And very sad," Ampata finished.

"Then talk to me," Xander implored her. "Let me know what's wrong."

"I can't." The girl dissolved into tears on his shoulder.

"Hey, I know why you can't tell me." Xander held her gently, trying to comfort her. "It's a secret, right? And if you told me, you'd have to kill me."

Spike groaned silently. No wonder the poor slob was hooked on a dead girl. Xander was humor-and-tact-challenged, which no doubt killed his chances with the live ones.

"Oh," Xander said lamely. "That was . . . a bad joke. And the delivery was off too. I'm sorry. I, uh—" He pulled back and wiped a tear off Ampata's cheek. "I'm sorry."

Spike winced when Xander kissed the girl, tentatively, then with more passion until suddenly the boy's whole body stiffened. Spike expected to see young, vibrant Xander wrinkle and dehydrate right before his eyes. Instead, Ampata pushed him away and he fell to the ground.

"No, I can't." The girl dropped down beside the gasping boy. "Xander, I'm so sorry." She held him for a moment, then looked up suddenly. "The seal."

Startled when Ampata ran off, Spike glanced at the boy lying on the floor. Xander was out of breath and too weak to move, an easy mark. *Easy to bag, but too much trouble to tote.* Spike didn't want to drag Dru's dinner across town or wait until Xander could walk on his own. Besides, the Slayer was rushing backstage.

Spike ducked behind a massive speaker before Buffy spotted him. As she ran by with Willow, he could smell the blood coursing hot through their veins. Exactly what Dru craved, but he wasn't looking for a fight tonight.

Spike detoured past the mall on his way back to the factory, hunting anyone handy.

Sunnydale
September 2002

Spike heard Buffy's footsteps receding down the corridor and glanced at the storeroom door. It was open. Anyone could get in: students, teachers, construction workers, even disgruntled dead people. Frantic, he grabbed the handle and pulled the door closed—hard. The sound disrupted the fog shrouding his mind, and his thoughts cleared.

For how long? He wondered, panicked. There was something he needed to know. Something important. Think!

"A predator doesn't think." *Adam* stood by the opposite wall, his massive arms folded over his chest, his half-human face devoid of emotion. "He reacts on instinct, swiftly and without hesitation, picking off the weaker ones in a pack first. You should have taken the one called Willow when you had the chance."

"Hard to get at her neck through that bloody parka," Spike said. "Her chin barely cleared the fur trim."

"A savage would have ripped the parka to shreds," *Adam* countered.

"Yeah, and he'd be picking fur out of his teeth for a week." Spike squatted in the middle of the room. He didn't know how long the clarity would last and focused on the conversation with the demon hybrid for stability.

"An inadequate excuse." *Adam* stared, his black eyes cold and lightless. "I offered to make you savage again in exchange for the Slayer, but even then you had excuses, too many reasons why it couldn't be done."

"There was that little problem with her pals," Spike reminded him. "A slayer by herself is more than most super Bads can handle. A slayer with a loyal band of merry marauders is practically invincible."

Adam wasn't convinced. "Your emotions made you weak and ineffectual."

Spike wanted to reject that, but there was a kernel of truth in the engineered mutant's observation. He had been passionately in love with Drusilla. Then he had threatened to kill her to show Buffy how much he loved *her*.

"You told the Slayer I was your salvation." *Dru* smiled, her voice smooth and mellow; it was like warm caramel when she was pleased. "That I delivered you from mediocrity."

"Yes." Spike nodded, his smile sad. A century together, and Drusilla had never stopped surprising him. She had come to the crypt to save him from the chip.

"I wanted to make things right again," *Dru* said, "but you didn't want to be saved, puppet Spike with your Tinkertoy strings. Can't hunt. Can't hurt. Can't kill."

"Wired for pain," Spike said.

"The Slayer didn't even care about that, did she?" *Dru's* tone became brittle and accusing.

Spike felt his mental hold slipping. He buried his head in his arms and rocked.

"You were a killer, bash, slash, making things

dead, and then you crawled to her like a worm." *Dru* mocked him with a plea he had once made to Buffy. "'Just give me something. A crumb, the barest smidgen. Tell me someday, maybe . . . there's a chance.'"

Then *Dru* was *Buffy*, glaring at him, her words loaded with disdain. "The only chance you had with me was when I was unconscious."

"Don't!" Spike covered his ears and squeezed his eyes closed, but the Other was relentless in Its assault.

"What happened to you, Spike?" *Adam* asked.

Spike didn't know. Before he came to Sunnydale he had been able to suppress the emotional tendencies and feelings that made him vulnerable. Then everything had started to unravel.

Adam pressed. "You were a ruthless, cold-blooded beast too powerful to contain, pure in your ferocity. Where did you go wrong?"

Spike didn't have to think about that. His first mistake had been letting Buffy live on Parent-Teacher Night. His second mistake was getting to know her and her friends.

Sunnydale
October 1997

Since becoming a vampire, Spike's interest in academics had been restricted to stalking coeds on the happy hunting grounds of university campuses. On occasion he attended poetry seminars and readings, and his own poems, composed and saved in memory only, had improved over the years. He hadn't indulged in either pastime since arriving in Sunnydale. A sinister undercurrent permeated the grounds of UC Sunnydale. He couldn't name or identify what he sensed, but it discouraged hunting and stifled creative flow.

No such suffocating atmosphere depressed the allure of Crestwood College. With its rolling lawns, wooded paths, and Spanish architecture, the small, exclusive institution of higher learning invited investigation. Spike was looking forward to cruising the dorms, sororities, and frat houses after he finished with Professor Dalton.

The linguistics professor had been out of town for the past week, attending a rare-book-sellers convention and forcing Spike to put his search for the *du Lac Manuscript* on hold. He'd found out that Dalton kept late hours on Wednesdays for student conferences and faculty consultations, and Spike had an unscheduled appointment.

Dalton's office was located in a building that combined anthropology, archeology, archaic languages, and other studies related to ancient human history and development. No one roamed the quiet halls or waited in the corridor to see the professor. Spike entered the small, cluttered office without knocking and leaned against the doorjamb.

Dalton sat hunched over a wooden desk, reading a parchment with a magnifying glass. A short, mousy man with thin hair and glasses, he probably made up in brains what he lacked in stature and appeal. Nature had a built-in default for balance in all things.

"I stopped seeing people at—" The professor squinted at Spike over the top of his glasses. "Who are you?"

Spike didn't bother with an introduction or small talk. "Your friend Roman Shaw bought the *du Lac Manuscript* for a client a few weeks ago. Who's the client?"

"That's none of your business. Now—get out of my office." Frowning, the professor waved the magnifying glass toward the door. He jumped with a sharp intake of breath when Spike took a step forward and kicked the door closed.

"Quite the contrary," Spike said in a conversational tone. "I need that text to save someone near and dear to my heart, and that makes it my business." He vamped out and roared. "Who's the client?"

Professor Dalton dropped the magnifying glass. His mouth worked as he tried to talk, but no sound came out.

"Anytime in the next thirty seconds will be acceptable," Spike said. "I was going to grab someone to eat on my way home, but I can make do with a stringy, balding guy—if you get my meaning."

Dalton nodded and swallowed hard. "I don't know. Roman did—didn't tell me."

"Well, give him a ring and ask!" Spike exclaimed.

"He lives in London," Dalton said. "It's just before dawn there."

Spike leaned over and snarled. "Wake him up."

Dalton picked up the phone and dialed. "Hello,

Roman? Yes, yes. This is Martin Dalton. I realize it's early, but I have a rather urgent request."

"Very urgent," Spike muttered as he perched on the corner of the desk.

"This is a little irregular, but I really must know who bought the du Lac text." Dalton nodded vigorously and interrupted his friend. "Yes, I understand, but I have a contact who's, uh—willing to pay a hefty fee to see it. At the very least, your client should know."

Spike craned to see what Dalton scrawled on a notepad.

"Ah, he's not a wealthy chap, then?" Dalton nodded, smiled, and then blinked in surprise. "He's the what where? I never would have guessed. Yes, well, thanks so much."

"And the client is?" Spike prompted.

"The librarian at Sunnydale High," Dalton said as he finished writing and handed Spike the slip of paper. "Rupert Giles."

Chapter Six

Professor Dalton was stunned—but alive—when Spike left the building to explore the Crestwood College campus. Of course, the academic's status was subject to change, depending on the *du Lac Manuscript*. Finding the book was only the first phase of Spike's project to restore Drusilla's health. Next, he had to take possession of the book. Then, depending on the language Josephus du Lac had used, he might need someone to translate it. If so, the good professor could be changed into a brainy henchman to do the job. In the meantime, since something unexpected could happen regarding the book or Rupert Giles, Dalton might be needed again—alive.

Besides, although the Sunnydale police had a

peculiar nonchalance about the exceptional number of deaths and disappearances in town, it wouldn't be wise to raise any red flags. Roman Shaw lived too far away to kill, and the agent knew that Professor Dalton had inquired about the *du Lac Manuscript*. If Dalton turned up dead, Shaw might tell Rupert Giles that someone wanted the text—badly. A long shot, to be sure, but Spike wasn't willing to take the risk.

The book buyer's identity could not be dismissed as a coincidence, either. Spike mulled over the connections between the *du Lac Manuscript*, Rupert Giles, and the Slayer as he walked through the Crestwood College campus. Several paths branched off a central courtyard toward the theater, academic facilities, student union, dorms, and fraternity row. Spike paused to read a signpost.

Three young men passed by without casting even a curious glance in Spike's direction. They were all dressed in a casual Ivy League style: slacks and button-down shirts with V-neck sweaters or blazers. Spike followed them toward the dorms, out of sight in the trees that lined the path, eavesdropping with mild interest.

"So Brian Randolph wasn't asked to pledge Delta Zeta Kappa either?" the tallest man asked.

"They only take guys from old money and/or old families," his heavyset companion explained. "Brian's father was an accountant before he became a dot-com millionaire."

"New wealth buys your way into Crestwood, Cory," the third man said, "but not into Crestwood's version of Skull and Bones."

"Don't they ever make exceptions?" Cory frowned.

"Not very often." The heavy man shrugged. "Why cut a stranger in on the wealth and success that's practically guaranteed to everyone in the house?"

"There's no 'practically' about it," the third man remarked with a shake of his head. "Those guys keep getting richer, and none of them ever go broke. Must be nice to have connections."

Indeed, Spike thought. Cory didn't have a prayer of crashing the rich boys' campus club. It was a familiar story: The offspring of wealth and privilege thought they were better than everyone else, and everyone else went along with the myth, creating a vicious cycle of power and abuse. Prompted by an old prejudice of his own, Spike left the students and headed toward fraternity row.

The Delta Zeta Kappa house didn't look anything like the fraternities Spike had hunted in in other parts of the country. Instead of a stately mansion on a tree-lined street, the frat was a sprawling hacienda set in the middle of an expansive green meadow. Wide steps led up to three arches that framed a large front porch. Several windows opened onto a balcony above the porch.

Spike studied the structure from the woods that bordered the drive and parking area. There was no movement behind the windows and doors. Assuming the members were all watching TV or studying, he started to leave. But the sound of breaking glass drew him back.

A girl plunged through an upstairs window onto the balcony and scrambled over the wall. As she dropped to the ground, a figure in a brown hooded robe dashed through the broken glass. As soon as the robed figure realized the girl wasn't on the second floor, he ran back inside. The girl stumbled to her feet and started running. She had barely gone twenty yards when five robed figures dashed out of the house and took off after her.

"If I had known there was going to be entertainment, I would have brought popcorn." Intrigued, Spike followed at a discreet distance.

The girl headed into the woods at the southern end of the house and stumbled just before she reached the high stone wall that surrounded the school. Getting quickly to her feet, she climbed onto a low curved tree trunk and hoisted herself up and over the wall—right into the cemetery.

To avoid the boys in monks' clothing, Spike scaled the wall farther down and kept pace as they barreled across a paved drive. As they started to close ground, a young man with sandy-blond hair, who had circled around, stopped the girl.

She screamed, anguished and frightened when he grabbed her wrists.

Spike watched from behind a large grave marker. The scene didn't impress a vampire who had stalked, captured, and killed women all over the world. He had an impulsive streak, but the boys were crude.

"Callie, Callie . . ." The young man smiled, amused by the girl's struggles. "Where you going?"

Callie sobbed pitifully.

"The party's just getting started." The college boy

in the monk suit shoved her into the clutches of three other robed figures. As they dragged her back toward the Delta Zeta Kappa house, the man stole a furtive glance around, then pulled up his hood and followed.

Spike leaned against the tombstone, shaking his head. He was a demon. It was his job to terrify, torture, and kill people. Humans had souls, which made their evil transgressions more disgusting and vile somehow, especially rich brats trying to run with the Big Bads for kicks.

Spike frowned, recalling that the members of Delta Zeta Kappa enjoyed a remarkable degree of financial success. It was quite possible that a demonic Big Bad was the boys' Big Boss.

Leaving Drusilla behind on Thursday night wasn't a problem. Yesterday, after the monk-boys had left the cemetery with the girl, Spike had found a nest and ambushed a blackbird sitting on her eggs. With the bird firmly in hand, he had nicked a cage and some packaged seed from a local pet store. Dru had adored the gift and was content to stay home, singing to her feathered captive.

Some of his underlings hadn't been as cooperative.

"What do you mean, 'they're gone?'" Spike glared at Lucius. Vampires operated pretty much with impunity in Sunnydale, but nothing prevented the oddball mayor or chief of police from cracking down on "violent crime" without notice. Spike had instituted strict rationing until Dru's cure was complete, and had relied on Lucius to enforce it. "I gave specific orders. Everyone has to wait their turn."

"I tried to stop them," Lucius said, "but Hank was hungry."

"A vampire doesn't need to feed every night! I went without a drop for weeks once." Spike's eyes blazed. "Hank has an eating disorder! He only *thinks* he's hungry."

"But Drusilla feeds every night." Lucius cringed, as though he expected Spike to lash out.

Spike held his temper rather than draw attention to Drusilla's weakening condition. He had enough to do without worrying that an ambitious subordinate might try to get to him through her. This new discipline problem was a distraction he could have done without.

"I'll deal with Hank when I get back," Spike said.

Lucius smiled, imagining the worst for Hank and savoring the prospects. "What about Dorian and Garbo?"

Dorian and Garbo hadn't made trouble before, but they had gone hunting with Hank, a defiance Spike couldn't ignore. He glanced back at Lucius as he headed for the factory door. "They better hope I don't have any trouble checking a book out of the library."

Spike kept to alleys and side streets as he made his way through Sunnydale to the high school campus. Traffic and pedestrian activity was heavy for a weeknight, and Main Street cafés filled up as downtown specialty shops closed. From the looks of the crowds clogging the sidewalks, business had been brisk.

Spike's predatory instincts were primed when he reached the Sunnydale High School grounds. The surveillance mission was more critical than an ordinary hunt, and he scanned the parking lot before he strode across it. Since three cars were parked in the faculty section, he assumed three adults were still on the premises. Teachers or janitors would be working and easily avoided, especially the old duffer who drove the broken down Citroen DS. He didn't want to create a commotion that would hinder his search for the *du Lac Manuscript*.

The only positive result of his botched attempt to kill the Slayer on Parent-Teacher Night was that he knew the location of the library. With Dru's life depending on his efforts, he proceeded with more caution than usual. He had planned to scout the library through the windows first, but the two semicircular windows with a view of the interior were too high to access from the ground.

Having no recourse but to learn the library's layout from the inside, Spike continued on around the building. As long as he was on a reconnaissance outing, he might as well recon everything.

If Spike hadn't been studying the high school structure, he wouldn't have seen the boarded-up break in the foundation. He swung the loose boards aside and stepped through a narrow opening into a dark cellar with a low ceiling. His eyes quickly adjusted. Nothing of value was stored in the space, but empty paint cans, pieces of lumber, and other discarded construction debris were strewn about the dirt floor.

Footsteps overhead drew Spike's gaze to a faint sliver of light shining through a narrow wooden door at the top of ladderlike stairs. He waited until the footsteps retreated, then silently climbed up. The door was actually a hatch that opened into an area filled with floor-to-ceiling bookshelves.

Realizing he had stumbled on a secret way into the library, Spike considered his next step before entering. If the back stacks were any indication, the high school library was exceptionally large and well stocked. If the librarian was clever, he had hidden the *du Lac Manuscript* in plain sight among thousands of other volumes.

Spike stifled his natural inclination to storm the stacks and take Giles prisoner. He could torture the librarian into revealing the location of the book, but if Giles died without telling, the *du Lac Manuscript* might be lost. Then Dru would die too. The seize-and-brutalize option was best saved as a last resort, in the event all else failed.

The librarian was obviously working late tonight, but Spike doubted Giles was on the job twenty-four/seven. Although it went against his impulsive grain, he knew a methodical search in an unoccupied library was a better plan.

But as long as I'm here, it can't hurt to take a quick look. Spike eased inside and crept to the end of the stacks.

The back section of the library, where Spike was standing, was raised four feet off the main floor. A railing of spindles and posts ran the length of the platform, and a wide staircase led down from an open space under the semicircular windows. Study tables with chairs and bankers' lamps dominated the lower floor.

An office and checkout counter filled the space on the left. The double doors he remembered from Parent-Teacher Night were directly across the room. A green-lighted exit sign hung above them. Also: a clock, bulletin board, planter, card catalog, and locked wire door into a small room with more books.

Books the librarian doesn't want anyone to see, Spike thought, as a tall man walked out of the office carrying a book. *Rupert Giles, I presume.*

The man looked like a librarian, with glasses, a slightly receding hairline, vest, and proper tie. The book in his hand was an ordinary volume, not the one Spike was looking for.

"I dare say I'm the only Watcher that's ever been assigned to a slayer with a social life." Giles mumbled as he walked to the study table and slapped the book onto one of several stacks needing to be reshelved. "Who could have imagined such a thing?"

I certainly didn't, Spike thought. He had suspected Rupert Giles might be Buffy's Watcher. An ordinary school librarian wouldn't buy a one-of-a-kind volume of evil rituals and spells or keep it around for young, impressionable eyes to browse. That Giles would be British was pretty much a given.

"'Seven to seven-oh-five.'" The librarian huffed. "As though she doesn't abandon her training and duties whenever she has something else she'd rather do."

Spike had also suspected that Buffy's independent streak was difficult to manage. It was fun knowing the straight-laced old wanker disapproved of the girl's gregarious lifestyle. They had something in common, actually—both in charge of escape artists. Hank was getting on *his* nerves too.

"I suppose I should be thankful she doesn't complain about her nightly cemetery patrols." Sighing, Giles slid the top six books off the stack into his arms. As he started up the stairs to put them away, Spike slipped back into the cellar.

Now that he had a way to get in and out of the library undetected, Spike could look for the *du Lac Manuscript* without fear of being caught or having his purpose discovered. He replaced the loose boards over the hole in the foundation and continued on around the building, looking for any other anomalies that might prove helpful.

Spike didn't find anything else unusual, but when he rounded the corner of the building, he saw Giles walking toward the parking lot. Apparently, the librarian had left most of the stacked books to be put away in the morning. Spike almost laughed aloud when the Brit stopped by the old Citroen and reached in his trouser pocket for his keys. The Watcher didn't notice the three forms waiting at the edge of the pavement on the far side of the lot, but Spike did.

Hank, Dorian, and Garbo were about to attack Giles.

"Bloody hell." Spike cursed under his breath.

Speeding unseen across the dark campus, Spike tackled Hank just as the minion made his move. As he and Hank fell, Spike grabbed Dorian's ankle and yanked him off his feet. Garbo stopped dead and stared. Spike closed his hand around a small tree branch on the ground, jumped back to his feet, and planted a boot on Hank's chest before Dorian had figured out what happened. "Do not move," Spike said quietly, fuming. He snapped the branch in half, creating a crude but lethal stake.

Nobody moved.

While Spike waited for Giles to get his stubborn car started, he reviewed his options. The three underlings had blatantly defied his authority. Although he couldn't afford to deplete the lower ranks, the crime could not go unpunished.

As soon as the Citroen turned out of the parking lot and lurched down the street, Spike pressed down harder on Hank's chest.

"Who gets to meet the big feather duster in the sky first?" Spike held the stake at ready. "None of you were scheduled to feed tonight. So what the hell are you doing out here?"

Garbo glanced down at Dorian, but she was too frightened to answer.

"We haven't fed in two days," Hank said. He was full of bluster despite the boot on his breastbone and the stake aimed at his heart. "You have no right to starve us, Spike."

If the minions had killed Rupert Giles, Spike would have lost his one solid link to the book that could save Drusilla's life. He was out of patience. With a speed the other vampires couldn't track, he dropped to one knee over Hank and drove the stake into his chest. He was back on his feet before the dust settled. "There, you won't starve now, Hank."

Before Dorian recovered from the shock, Spike was straddling his prone body with the stake pulled back to strike again. Hank had paid the price for disobedience. Spike just wanted to make sure the other two had gotten the point.

"How hungry are you, Dorian?" Spike asked.

"I'm good for another week." Dorian held his hands up, palms out. "Garbo and I were just out for a walk."

"Yeah, that's right." Garbo nodded vigorously and flipped her blond hair behind her shoulder. "Just walking, looking for something to do."

"Bored, eh?" Spike stood up and motioned Dorian to rise. "Well, I've got a job that will keep you both busy and out of trouble for a while. There's a book I want from the school library."

As he led Dorian and Garbo to the hidden hole in the foundation, Spike described the *du Lac Manuscript*. He gave them strict instructions, which they both swore to follow: Search only when the library was empty and don't kill anyone enrolled in, working at, or otherwise connected to the high school. In return he would give them permission to hunt every night at the mall.

Prompted by Giles's remarks, Spike went looking for Buffy before going back to the factory. He knew she was patrolling one of Sunnydale's many cemeteries. Although it was efficient to execute vampires the moment they rose from the grave, the newly undead wouldn't begin to task the Slayer's skills. Still, he might learn something useful.

Spike spotted Buffy strolling through the tombstones of the third Sunnydale cemetery he scouted, the one that bordered Crestwood College. The Slayer paused near the spot where the monk-boys had grabbed the girl the night before. He hung back when she knelt to pick up a piece of shiny metal, and resisted the urge to trade insults and lob a few threats.

The Slayer would dance with him soon, but right now he was more interested in watching her work. A wise warrior knew the enemy.

Sunnydale
September 2002

That had been the first—but not the last time Spike had used the "know your enemy" excuse for not killing Buffy. Learning about his opponents gave him a psychological edge in the final contest.

He had rushed blindly into his fight with the Chinese slayer, knowing nothing about her or her skills. Killing the girl had been exhilarating, but not as satisfying as killing Nikki. He had stalked Nikki, and then tormented her with threats against her son before taking her life.

"You came to know your enemy too well," *Adam* said. The massive hybrid paced the small basement storeroom.

Spike squatted in the middle of the floor with his arms wrapped around himself, rocking slightly, trying to ignore the apparitions that taunted him.

"It wasn't the chip or stinkin' luck that kept you

from killing the Slayer," *Adam* said, following up on a conversation they had had almost three years before. "You did fear her."

"Yes," Spike said, hoping his admission would make *Adam* declare victory and fade away.

"Why?" *Adam* asked. "She was just a girl."

"A girl who could drive a stake through my heart," Spike said.

Buffy knelt down in front of him. "That wasn't it, though, was it, Spike?"

"No." He shook his head. That had never been it. He hadn't been afraid of her at all, not until he started to love her. Then he was afraid she wouldn't love him back, wouldn't need him.

"I never need you, Spike." *Buffy* smiled, knowing the words hurt more than a stake and the nothing of oblivion. "And I could never trust you enough for it to be love."

Spike buried his face in his arms. He didn't want to listen, but the past was immutable, and the truth burned—scorching hot and seared in bitter memory. Buffy couldn't trust him because he had forced himself on her and called it love. He had gotten the spark back to fix himself—for her, but that wasn't enough. It didn't change what he had been and done, and couldn't make her understand.

"I had a speech," Spike said. "I learned it all. Oh, God, she won't understand. She won't understand." The magnitude of the truth was crushing. He raked his fingers through his hair, but the throbbing pain could not be soothed.

"Of course she won't understand, Sparky." *Warren*

walked behind him. "*I'm* beyond her understanding."

Once, the mad teenage scientist's superior attitude and caustic words had annoyed Spike. It no longer mattered.

"She's a girl!" *Warren* sputtered with the unguarded contempt of the rejected and reviled.

Spike had never been able to ignore the fact that Buffy was a girl.

Sunnydale
October 1997

Spike leaned against the trunk of a shade tree at the edge of the cemetery drive, taking the Slayer's measure from the perspective of one who could and would destroy her. He had already confirmed that she was as strong, quick, and skilled as the slayers before her. But Buffy had something extra, a definitive identity that defied her calling and, consequently, enhanced it. The very things that disturbed her Watcher's sense of order in the realm of Slayerhood made Buffy more than her destiny expected.

Buffy was the ultimate trophy, the kill that would change Spike's story into a legend. But because she was that good, he had to know her to kill her.

Spike suspected that Buffy wore her hair clipped high on her head because she liked the way it looked, not because she could fight better with her blond locks tied out of the way. The light blue sweater with the plunging *V* neckline begged her demonic opponents to underestimate her and dared the oh-so-serious Giles to object. Spike's brow knit in consternation as Buffy studied the bracelet she had found in the grass. Even he had been distracted by her good looks and perky personality once, but it wouldn't happen again.

"There's blood on it."

Buffy jumped up, startled by the sound of Angelus's voice.

Bollocks, Spike thought with a grimace. He had felt violently ill when his henchmen told him that the once renowned Angelus now called himself Angel. He had been too busy to investigate the returning-soul phenomenon, but that bit of voodoo was at the top of his find-out-ASAP list.

Of even greater interest now was why the Slayer didn't whip out a stake and dust the abomination. Angel *was* still a vampire.

"Hi," Buffy said, surprised by the sneak verbal attack but apparently not upset that Angel was the intruder. "It's nice to—blood?"

"I can smell it," Angel explained.

"Oh." The Slayer swallowed, looking disturbed and disgusted.

Disturbed and disgusted because Angel could smell blood, Spike wondered, or because she was having a friendly conversation with a vampire? Watching them, he suspected he'd be disturbed and disgusted by the answer.

"It's pretty thin," Buffy went on. "Probably belonged to a girl."

"Probably," Angel replied.

The running girl from last night, perhaps, Spike thought. He hadn't considered the fate of the terrified young thing the snob frat boys had kidnapped. However, it was a sure bet they hadn't dragged her back to the hacienda for tea and cartoons.

Buffy hesitated, playing with the bracelet. Then she laughed nervously to cover the awkward pause. "I—I was just thinking—wouldn't it be funny—" She shrugged self-consciously. "—sometime to see each other when it wasn't a blood thing."

Oh, God, no! Spike staggered back a step as the meaning of the scene suddenly sank in. The Slayer was making a bloody play for Angel!

Apparently Angel was staggered too. He didn't say anything.

The Slayer quickly tried to fill the uncomfortable void. "Not funny ha-ha."

"What're you saying?" Angel asked with a not-taking-this-seriously inflection in his voice. "You want to have a date?"

Spike rolled his eyes and covered his face with his hand. It was inconceivable that two definitive icons of the perpetual struggle between good and evil were flirting—badly—and making goo-goo eyes at each other in a cemetery.

"No," Buffy said, too quickly to mean it.

"You don't want a date?" Angel sounded puzzled.

"Who said date?" The Slayer backed off. "I—I never said date."

"Right," Angel agreed. "You just want to have coffee or something."

"Coffee?" Buffy winced.

"I knew this was going to happen," Angel said.

Spike shook his head. He had thought nothing could make him more contemptuous of Angel than knowing he had gone over to the good guys, but he had been wrong. The Slayer was throwing herself at Angel, the once Dark Prince of all that was unholy, and Angel was pushing her away.

"What?" The Slayer looked torn between anxiety and relief. "What do you think is happening?"

"You're sixteen years old. I'm two hundred forty-one."

"I've done the math," Buffy countered.

"You don't know what you're doing. You don't know what you want—" Angel glanced away.

Spike recognized the tone. Angelus had been a fine lady-killer, charming and feeding on beautiful women from Paris to Babylon. Angel had sworn off the feeding part, but he dismissed Buffy and her feelings as though the idea of them together was too ridiculous to consider. To the Slayer's credit, she got the message.

"Oh, no. I think I do," Buffy said. "I want out of this conversation."

"Listen." Angel grabbed Buffy's arm as she tried to brush past him. "If we date, we both know that one thing's going to lead to another."

Angel was no longer dithering around, teasing the girl to boost his masculine ego. He was grim and earnest. Spike's initial revulsion regarding the romantic angle was replaced by an intense interest in the Slayer's response.

"One thing already has led to another," Buffy said. "Don't you think it's a little late to be reading me the warning label?"

Buffy's expression was grave, but her eyes brimmed with a longing Spike hadn't felt in a long time. He had looked at Cecily with the same unconditional adoration, and then Drusilla, after she had captured his heart and affection. He and Dru were bound by a love of ages, but the white-hot intensity of new love had faded some of late. He had thought Dru's failing health to blame, but perhaps time was at fault.

"I'm just trying to protect you," Angel said. "This could get out of control."

"Isn't that the way it's supposed to be?" Buffy asked.

Yes, it is, Slayer, Spike thought. Great love burned with a dangerous, consuming flame, and eons of time could not extinguish the fires of such passion. He and Dru had loved with a fury no human girl, not even a slayer, could possibly match.

The Slayer gasped when the vampire clenched his teeth and pulled her close. As tight as Angel's grip was on her arms, the force that bound their eyes was stronger.

"This isn't some fairy tale," Angel told her. "When I kiss you, you don't wake up from a deep sleep and live happily ever after."

"No," Buffy said. "When I kiss you, I want to die." She held his gaze for a profound second, then turned and ran.

Spike watched her go, stunned by the power of her

words. As he melted into the darkness, away from Angel and the passion the Slayer had aroused, he lapsed into sober contemplation of the unexpected development.

What kind of slayer was attracted to a vampire? Angelus may have gotten his soul back and changed his name, but he had defiled, tormented, and brutally murdered thousands of innocent people. The question had to be answered if Spike hoped to understand this girl, one of the few in her generation to be empowered to kill his kind. He had defeated two slayers, one because he knew what mattered more to her than her own life.

Buffy was a dangerous enigma.

Disturbed by the hold she suddenly had on his thoughts, Spike glanced in the direction she had gone.

"Better beware, Slayer," Spike said, intrigued by a kill scenario he had not considered before. "If I kiss you, you *will* die."

Chapter Seven

Spike ducked when Miss Martha's head flew off. The porcelain missile missed him and broke into pieces on the wall. Sawdust stuffing spewed from the headless body as Dru continued to smash the doll against the bedpost. The novelty of the bird had already worn off, and she was angry because Spike wouldn't take her out tonight.

Dru stopped suddenly and cradled the broken remnants of the doll in her arms. "Poor Miss Martha. She got in the way of the tempest, and not even the king's men can put the Humpty Dumpty dolly together again."

Fearing another eruption, Spike chose his words carefully. "Perhaps we should give Miss Martha a proper burial, then—have a funeral and all."

Dru slowly turned her head, slicing him with a dark scowl. "But there's no one to come and pay their respects. All the mourners will be at the party."

"I'm only assuming the Delta Zeta Kappa boys are having a party. They *are* a fraternity, and it *is* Friday." Even if they were, Spike had to check out his demonic Big Boss theory before he decided to take the minions hunting at Crestwood. He had made the mistake of hypothesizing out loud, which prompted Dru's tantrum. "What if we cremate Miss Martha on a funeral pyre with a ceremony tomorrow?"

Dru nodded, then smiled. "Miss Martha would like that, but you'll have to bring her mummy a condolences present." Her eyes were hard on him again. "Because it's your fault mummy smashed the baby all to bits."

Back on familiar ground now, Spike relaxed. He walked over and put his arms around her. "What would you like, pet?"

"The last one the minions brought me for dinner was old and stringy," Dru said. "His blood was moldy."

"A gourmet student, then," Spike suggested, "from a fine, exclusive school. Girl or boy?"

"I want a mother." Dru tilted her head coyly. "A hot-blood who'll struggle before I kill her. The Slayer's mother."

"The Slayer's mother?" Spike frowned. "The Slayer's mum who popped me with an axe?"

"Yes, that one." Dru reached for a basket on the crate behind her and put the broken doll body inside. "Everybody's had a special mother except me."

"Who has?" Spike asked sharply, assuming she meant the henchmen.

"Angelus killed my mother," Dru said. "I was behind a curtain and saw him do it." She knelt to pick up the pieces of the porcelain doll's head and the green ribbon gag.

"He was a heartless rogue, wasn't he?" Spike hadn't told her yet that Angelus was now Angel, a vampire with a soul.

"You killed your own mother right before my eyes, didn't even give me a taste," Dru said as she placed the shattered doll's head in the basket. Then she muttered, sneering softly, "Take her with us to lay waste to Europe."

"Will you never let me forget it?" The memory of his mother always evoked an unbridled anger, but Spike immediately regretted the outburst. Drusilla only mentioned it when she was extraordinarily vexed, as she was now. "You should have a mother. It's the least I can do."

"Yes, you've been neglecting me lately," Dru said. "I deserve a special treat."

"The mall probably has a lovely selection." Spike wanted to grant her wish, but he balked at sending the Slayer an invitation to come after him before Dru was restored.

"I'll have the Slayer's mum." Dru fixed him with her dark gaze, not imploring or demanding but set. Her mind was made up. Peace and quiet at the factory would end for the foreseeable future unless he gave in.

He gave in.

Appeased and happy, Dru set about cleaning up the sawdust, evidence of Miss Martha's untimely destruction.

Spike had no trouble finding Buffy's house. Sunnydale vampires made a point of knowing the location so they could avoid the Slayer's neighborhood. The modest two-story home sat midblock on a tree-lined residential street. A front walk paralleled a narrow driveway and led up to a wide porch. A house-shaped mailbox stood by the curb.

"Summers." Spike read the wood-burned sign attached to the mailbox post and glanced at the house. A car was in the drive, but no one was visible in the lighted front windows. He opened the mailbox and withdrew two bills waiting for pickup tomorrow. According to the return address, Buffy's mother's name was Joyce.

"May she rest in peace," Spike muttered, replacing the mail and closing the box.

He made a quick circle of the property, trying to determine if Buffy was home and taking in details that might be useful when he finally put his mind and energies to killing her. The layout was similar to a hundred other houses he had cased since coming to America: living room, kitchen, and dining room on the ground floor, bedrooms and bath on the top, and a full basement. He leaned over to look in the small window at ground level and rubbed dirt away with his coat sleeve. The area under the house was unfinished, held the usual washer and dryer, and served as a storage dump.

Spike didn't have much taste for the task at hand and just wanted to get it done. He hated being manipulated, even by Dru, but domestic tranquility was essential if he wanted to function in top form.

As Spike passed by the back door, he heard the phone ring. He moved closer to the door as Joyce picked up in the kitchen.

"Where are you, Buffy?" Joyce asked, and then stiffened with surprise. "With Cordelia? Cordelia Chase?"

The evil social director of Sunnydale High, Spike thought with a grimace. His opinion of the Slayer dropped a few notches. She hadn't struck him as an in-crowd wannabe. She hung out with Willow and Xander.

"What kind of school project?" Joyce listened, then nodded. "Well, you are a junior. I guess it is time to start looking into colleges. Try not to be too late."

When Joyce went into the living room, Spike returned to the front of the house. Since Buffy wasn't home, he considered knocking on the door, but there wasn't much chance a slayer's mum would invite a stranger in or step outside. Joyce probably didn't know her teenage daughter moonlighted as a demon killer, but she would know that Sunnydale was full of unsavory elements. He found a secluded spot at the corner of the porch and settled in to wait. He had no intention of waiting all night, however. There was still the unsolved riddle of the monk-boys.

Spike knew a little something about young men, and sophisticated collegians didn't dress up as monks to impress sorority girls. They would only don such trappings to worship something, and only something evil would make it worth their while. Sunnydale was demon Disneyland, and the world had no shortage of fools who thought they could strike bargains with evil and win. According to the fraternity's rejects, Delta Zeta Kappa had a lock on good fortune. If the monk-boys were in league with a demonic Big Bad for profit, the gravy train would last awhile, but it wouldn't last forever.

And if Joyce didn't leave the house by nine so he could leave and confirm his theory, he'd have to go home to Dru empty-handed.

"Not looking forward to that," Spike mumbled with a sigh. He was anxiously awaiting the day when Dru would be able to hunt with wild abandon again. "Then she can kill her own bloody mothers."

Spike tensed at the sound of the front door opening and closing. He heard the jingle of car keys and the tap of heels on the paved walk. He would not be able to sweet-talk a sensible older woman into going with him. He'd have to knock Joyce out and carry her back to the factory, but at least the mommy debt Dru felt was owed her would be paid in full.

With interest, Spike thought when Joyce Summers moved into view beyond the hedge. She was attractive. Her posture was perfect without being stiff, and she carried herself with a quiet confidence that left no doubt where Buffy's faith in her own judgment and ability had come from. She held two DVD cases and was probably on her way to return them to the rental shop.

As Joyce inserted her key to unlock the car door, Spike poised to attack. When she opened the door and slid into the driver's seat, he was still poised to attack.

He relaxed when she slammed the door closed and started the engine.

Even demons had lines they wouldn't cross. Spike had just never confronted his subconscious, self-imposed limit before. He had killed women who had children, including the second slayer, Nikki. He had killed her because she was the Slayer.

Dru wanted Joyce Summers because she was the Slayer's mother. She meant for Buffy to suffer the same horrendous anguish Angelus had caused her. This time, however, Spike had to deny Dru's malicious desire to feed and inflict pain.

Joyce deserved to live for taking a whack at him with an axe, defending her young.

Spike shrugged as Joyce backed her car out of the driveway. A mother's unconditional love was one of the most powerful forces on Earth. His mother had been the only one to love and accept him for who he was before Dru changed him. He had no doubt that Buffy's mother loved her just as fiercely and completely. Mums were like that.

Invigorated and itching for a real fight, Spike headed toward Crestwood College. As he walked through the cemetery, his high spirits were dampened by a recollection of the previous night. He still hadn't digested the nauseating fact that Angel and Buffy were on a romantic fast track spring-loaded with physical and emotional tension. His only consolation regarding Angelus's plummet from black grace was that a relationship between a vampire and a slayer would come to no good end—eventually. In the meantime he had to get rid of the vile taste the whole sordid scene had left in his mouth.

Blood was the only remedy.

Spike scaled the college's southern wall and dropped into the woods that bordered the Delta Zeta Kappa fraternity house. No guards prowled the grounds, and he crossed the open lawn in seconds. However, a man had been posted on the veranda outside the front door. Rather than announce his intentions with a dead doorman, Spike scouted the outside of the building. An arched window off the kitchen was open, and his first question was answered the instant he climbed through. The frat house was a demon lair: no invitation necessary.

A cursory scan of the large kitchen on his left confirmed his party hypothesis too. The counters were stacked with champagne flutes, cocktail glasses, napkins, crackers, toothpicks for canapés, and serving trays. Tubs of ice filled with bottled beer sat on the floor.

A delivery invoice was tacked to the message board on the wall. Tom Warner had purchased and signed for the shipment of imported beer and champagne.

"But where are the bloody brats?" Spike peered over the counter in front of the window. The interior décor was a combination of New World Spanish and silver and black bachelor chic. Framed prints and photographs shared wall space with wooden Spanish-style sconces. The furniture was heavy and sparse. Nothing outstanding caught Spike's eye. Then he heard the muffled sound of chanting through the door on his right. He cracked it open.

"I pledge my life and my death to the Delta Zeta Kappas and to Machida, whom we serve."

Machida? Spike blinked. He recognized the oath of loyalty, except that the last time he'd heard someone take the vow, it had been to Machida and the von Hardt family.

Spike eased the door open wider. The flickering light of lanterns created a pattern of light and dark on the walls of carved stone, and the air stank with the pungent odor of something foul or dead. A stone staircase led down into the damp grotto where a gathering of robed boys tempted fate in order to reap the rewards of a mediocre demonic power.

What were they keeping on ice in the red cooler? Spike wondered. The insulated box on the landing was completely out of place in the medieval underground setting.

"On my oath, before my assembled brethren," another man said.

The first voice repeated the words. "On my oath, before my assembled brethren."

The fraternity was deep into an induction ritual that had probably lasted most of the day. Spike knew the drill. The man being inducted was naked to the waist with his hands clasped behind his back.

Machida's servant pressed the tip of a sword into the pledge's chest. "I promise to keep our secret from this day until my death."

"I promise to keep our secret from this day until my death." The pledge dutifully repeated the words.

"In blood I was baptized, and in blood I shall reign, in his name."

Spike muffled a snort of contempt as the pledge echoed back the words. Machida hadn't lost his flair for the melodramatic, but compared to a vampire, the overgrown reptile was as bloodthirsty as a bunny.

"You are now one of us," Machida's man said.

"In his name!" the pledge shouted.

"In his name!" several voices repeated.

"Brewski time!" the man in charge announced.

"Party!" someone else yelled.

Rock music blared, and a Machida monk raced up to the red cooler. Spike closed the door and ducked back out the window. He had no doubt now as to the fate of the girl they had captured last night. It was time for Machida's annual meal of luscious young ladies.

And what perfect timing it is, Spike thought with a grin as he sped into the woods and back over the wall. The demonic event was even better cover for his hungry horde than he had dared hope. No matter how many students the vampires killed in the vicinity of the Delta Zeta Kappa house, Machida's cult of fraternity boys would take the blame. He certainly didn't owe the lazy snake-fiend anything. *Quite the opposite was true.*

Atlantic Ocean
1943

Spike kept one eye on the eastern horizon behind him as he swam for the New England shore. Angelus had put him and Ensign Sam Lawson off the German submarine twenty miles off the coast, with eight hours of darkness. He had lost track of time. The sky was still pitch-black, but dawn was imminent, and he had no idea how close he was to making landfall.

He and Lawson, the new vampire Angelus had sired to save the ship, had parted company after five minutes together in the water. Spike had bid him good riddance. It wasn't Spike's fault the ensign and his American crew had been stranded four hundred feet down with three vampires, dead engines, and four German destroyers dropping depth charges. It was the Americans' fault for stealing the prototype sub from the Germans, and the Germans' fault for wanting to destroy the boat before the Americans learned its secrets.

It was also the Germans' fault that he and two other vampires had been on board.

Spike should have taken the cruise ship back to New York with Drusilla the year before, but he had stayed behind to pack and store the priceless treasures she had accumulated from desperate people fleeing Hitler's followers. Word had it that the Allies would overrun Europe in a year. He had thought that he had plenty of time to finish his business before returning to New York and Dru. No one had suspected the Nazis would begin rounding up demons and hauling them off to places unknown. He had almost been caught in a sweep of the Hamburg docks. . . .

Germany
1942

Spike frantically burrowed into the small cave. The drizzling rain that soaked the countryside during the night had cleared. He had a fighting chance against the Waffen-SS if they caught him. He had no chance if he was caught out in the morning sun.

Pebbles cut into Spike's knees as he wedged his body into the hillside and drew in his feet. If his boots caught fire, he wouldn't be able to move to extinguish the flames. At least he didn't have to breathe. His body blocked the flow of air into the cramped space.

But the two bullet holes in his leg hurt like hell.

Resting for the first time in hours, Spike assessed his unexpected reversal of fortune. He had heard rumors about demons, especially vampires, disappearing with no trace. He hadn't given the stories any credence until the SS soldier with the dog had found him feeding on a young merchant marine. The SS soldier had been inspecting ships, looking for one bound out of German-occupied territory.

Spike had run, leaving most of his bankroll and the key to Dru's vault behind. Losing the money made leaving the country more difficult, but he wouldn't miss the cumbersome loot. One of the many reasons he and Dru had survived for so long was their freedom from material baggage. It had taken a while to convince her that Angelus's and Darla's desire for luxurious surroundings endangered them. After he promised to replace everything she had to abandon when they moved, she had accepted the wisdom of traveling light. That was one rule he wouldn't break again, no matter how long she pouted.

A deep voice spoke German words.

Spike recognized the voice of the SS Colonel

Jürgen Koch, who was in charge of the hunting party searching the docks. The man's every word was uttered with crisp authority and obeyed without hesitation or question. Spike didn't speak German, but he understood enough words to get the gist of most conversations. Colonel Koch wanted to know where he was. Another man replied.

If Spike's sketchy translation was correct, the dogs had lost his scent and the SS officers thought he had burned up in the sun.

Spike smiled in spite of the deadly situation. The Nazis had pursued him throughout the night. The fresh bullet wounds had slowed him down and helped the dogs follow his scent in spite of the intermittent downpours. He had mustered a burst of speed half an hour ago and moved from puddle to puddle to hide his scent. Now, covered in dirt, with the bullet holes already starting to heal, he hoped the dogs would not be able to pick up his trail.

The Colonel's voice faded as he moved away.

His pursuers had given up, Spike realized. He prided himself on his irreverent arrogance and took some satisfaction in knowing the SS colonel thought he was smarter than other vampires. However, luck as much as cunning had saved him this time. He just hoped his luck held out. Since the SS had the ports covered, escaping the Third Reich by boat wasn't possible.

At sunset, Spike headed south toward Switzerland.

Chapter Eight

Bavaria
1943

The journey to Bavaria took months. Spike avoided cities and towns and the Nazi forces that had slithered into every segment of German society. He hid in the forests, fed on farmers, stole clothing and tools, and eluded Colonel Jürgen Koch and the Waffen-SS unit that had been tasked to hunt down and capture his kind.

Spike's luck had held, but only enough to keep him free. He was tired of running, of being dirty, and of eating men who were too old to fight in der Führer's army and women who were too old or too ugly for a German soldier to love. He wanted a hot bath, a soft bed, a radio, and a safe haven for more than one night. He wanted fresh, young blood.

The Bavarian mountains north of the Swiss border were rugged and riddled with caves, and Spike staked out a suitable daytime stopover before he went hunting. Since human fare was often scarce, he had grown grudgingly accustomed to deer, rabbit, and rodent blood out of necessity. He hadn't had a decent meal in over a week, and hunger was taxing his strength. He snared the first rabbit to cross his path with a lightning-fast hand. Then, fortified by the small animal's blood, he set out to find more substantial sustenance.

Spike abandoned the deer he was hunting when he stumbled upon the tracks of a sheep herd. Where there were sheep, there were bound to be shepherds. Staying hidden behind trees and boulders, he moved cautiously downhill to a ridge overlooking a long, narrow valley. A village and farms dotted the green meadows below, and an ancient castle stood in grim majesty on the cliff across the chasm. Then he realized his exploration had taken too long, and he was surveying the terrain in the gray light before dawn.

In danger of being caught out in the sun, Spike raced along the rimrock, looking for a cleft or cave. Desperate, as the edge of the fiery orb cleared the eastern mountain peaks, he jumped off the ridge. He landed in a hillside pasture strewn with large rocks, and rolled under an overhanging rock shelf just as the death rays touched his skin. His dark hair was singed and his ears sunburned when he settled into the nook of earth and stone to sleep.

Awakened by the sound of a girl's voice, Spike crawled to the edge of the rock shelter and peered out.

The sun was slowly sinking behind the western range.

A girl speaking German was coming toward him up the mountain, chasing a goat. Long golden braids tied with red ribbons bounced as she ran, and her laugh was like Christmas bells, pure and musical.

Spike looked downhill for a shepherd tending a herd, but no one else was in sight. He pinched his arm to be sure he wasn't dreaming. It had been too long since he had fed on the sweet blood of youth.

A hint of irritation marred the girl's sweet voice as she stumbled over a rock in the deepening twilight.

Spike's hunger burned, a fever in his veins.

The goat paused just out of the girl's reach and began to graze.

Spike crouched under the rock, watching the shadows lengthen, waiting until the last ray of lethal light was gone.

The girl took a rope from her apron pocket as she quietly approached the goat. The animal jumped and tried to run when she threw her arms around its neck, but she held on and slipped the noose over its head. Once captured, the goat stopped struggling and docilely followed as the girl started back down the slope.

Safe in the twilight gloom, Spike sprang. He grabbed the girl from behind and clamped a hand over her mouth before she could scream. She dropped the rope to claw his arm, and the goat bolted. Crazed by a starved bloodlust, Spike didn't feel the pain. The scent of terrified human erased everything else from his sphere of awareness. He yanked her golden braid, pulling her head over and exposing her neck, and roared as he bared his fangs.

Nothing could pierce Spike's frenzied need for blood. He was shocked to his senses when strong hands pulled him off the girl and threw him on the ground.

Spike scrambled to his feet, his knees wobbly from hunger. His eyes widened with indignant outrage when the girl started to run and a demon with bulging eyes and mottled frog skin pulled her back.

"Hey!" Spike yelled. "I saw her first."

A dwarf with curly dark hair handed the frog demon a wad of cloth to stuff in the screaming girl's mouth. As soon as the sound was muffled, the little guy shifted into vamp mode. The girl stared at his grotesque, misshapen visage for a full second before she passed out.

"We have orders to kill poachers," a large man said in heavily accented English. He planted himself in front of Spike, massive legs splayed, arms crossed, black eyes narrowed with belligerence.

"Taking a girl is called poaching around here?" Spike asked calmly. The slightest hint of fear might trigger an attack. Exhausted and weakened by hunger, he was outmatched.

The burly man was huge, with hard muscles and long hair twined with animal teeth, leather thongs, and wooden beads. He wore an animal-skin vest over a homespun shirt and carried a sword scabbard on his back. His ruddy complexion was too well preserved for him to be a two-thousand-year-old barbarian, but he looked exactly how Spike envisioned Attila the Hun.

The man nodded. "The young, pretty ones belong to Machida."

"But the demon master allows us to torment them before the ritual feast," the little man said. His British accent was refined, and he giggled insanely. Spike wondered if he had taught the large man to speak English, but didn't bother asking. It was a relief to find people who spoke his language.

"Trevor has his revenge whenever he can," the big man explained.

"Treated you like less than a man before the change, did they? I've done a bit of vengeance killing for that myself." Spike returned to human face and held his hand out to Trevor. "They call me Spike."

"Most pleased to make your acquaintance." Trevor shook his hand and bowed.

"Otto." The big man thumped his chest, then thumbed toward the frog demon holding the girl. "That's Pond."

Although he didn't let down his guard, Spike's alarm ebbed with the introductions. The trio had apparently been enlisted by the demon Machida to hunt and capture girls. However, since none of the three looked undernourished or unkempt, they obviously ate regularly and had a place to live that had running water. They were also roaming around free and fearless.

"So have the Nazis been through here yet?" Spike asked. "They've been cleaning out nests up north."

"We heard," Otto said, shrugging. "They won't bother us."

Spike couldn't tell if Otto's reply was based on

experience, conviction, or assumption. Right now, the fact that the SS wasn't combing the valley looking for demons was all he needed to know.

"So—is Machida hiring?" Spike asked, smiling.

As it turned out, Otto made the decisions regarding Machida's demon personnel and agreed to consider taking Spike on. Until he made up his mind, the newcomer would be welcome at Black Thorn Castle. The big man slung the girl over his shoulder and led the way down the rocky path.

Spike followed behind Otto with Trevor waddling at his heels. Pond brought up the rear. His long elastic tongue cracked each time he snapped a bug, small bird, or rodent into his mouth.

"How long have you been working for Machida?" Spike asked.

"Fifteen years," Trevor said, "but Otto's been in his service since the bloody snake moved into the castle four hundred and thirty-six years ago. It's just too delicious." He laughed hysterically and rubbed his chubby hands together.

"I was the groundskeeper for Helmet von Hardt when he struck the bargain with Machida," Otto said. "The family gives the demon reptile safe haven in the dungeon—and three girls a year—in exchange for perpetual prosperity."

"When did you become a vampire?" Spike knew that strange symbiotic relationships existed in the demon world, but usually vampires only served other vampires.

"Machida admired my strength," Otto explained,

"and had his favorite vampire wench change me that same night. I have never regretted it."

"Nor I," Spike admitted. "Until the past several months, it's been mostly fun and mayhem. But take my word for it, it's not easy being on the run from a whole bloody army."

"Or a mob," Trevor said. He stopped suddenly and began shrieking gibberish and yanking out tufts of his hair. After a moment, though, he continued on as though nothing odd had happened.

"I rescued the little bugger from a chalet on a hunting trip across the border," Otto said. "He amuses Machida, and he taught me the Queen's English. Earned his way."

"And Pond?" Spike glanced back. The mottled amphibian blended into the dark completely, but the odor of damp compost left no doubt he was still there.

"He earns his keep as well." Otto shifted the girl onto his other shoulder. "Black Thorn Castle is no longer swarming with pests."

But it's cold, damp, and drafty, Spike thought when they entered the fortress through a back portal.

Hung with heavy tapestries and renovated to incorporate modern conveniences, the structure was built of stone and mortar. The human family occupied most of the halls and chambers. As they walked, Otto told Spike that the villagers held Klaus von Hardt and his family in high esteem despite the disappearance of three teenage girls every year. Machida's influence extended beyond the castle to the hamlet, which had been built on von Hardt land and was thus entitled to a portion of the family's bounty. If anyone suspected a connection between the lost girls and the good fortune, they never whispered a word.

Machida's minions stayed on a level between the dungeon and the great hall. Although they lived apart from the humans, great care was given to the resident demons' basic needs and wants. The rooms were furnished for each individual's comfort, and everyone's required or preferred foods were available in abundance.

Except for human vampire fodder.

After Spike bathed and slept, Otto took him hunting in Switzerland. The Bavarian valley near the estate was Machida's private reserve and off-limits to the hired help. Although Spike resented the downgrade to servant status, it was far better than being dissected by Hitler's doctors or whatever horror the Nazis had planned for captive vampires.

After they crossed the border into neutral territory, Spike considered leaving Otto to continue his journey to Dru in America. Then Otto mentioned that Klaus von Hardt gave Machida's servants a share of his wealth after every annual feast. Otto had a hidden stash of diamonds, and Trevor had lucrative investments. It made sense to wait and gamble on von Hardt's generosity. Paying for passage on a luxury liner was preferable to stowing away on a merchant ship.

Machida and Klaus von Hardt agreed to let Spike stay on a trial basis. He would replace Pond on the hunting squad, leaving the amphibian free to exterminate insects and vermin from the castle premises full-time. A lower-level slug demon kept the walls and floor of the dungeon and Machida's den clean. There was also Peak, a shape-shifting panther with an exotic human form mortal men could not resist. She went with Otto, Trevor, and Spike to collect the third victim for Machida's imminent meal.

Spike slumped in the passenger seat of von Hardt's Mercedes-Benz as Otto steered down the winding mountain road toward the village. Trevor sat in the back seat with Peak, who was in human form for the outing.

"Is there something special about this new bird we're after?" Spike asked. The three vampires had ambushed the second girl on her way home from choir practice with no trouble a few nights before. "Why do we need the shape-shifter?" He twisted to look back. "No offense, Peak. Just curious."

Peak smiled, and Spike could not stop staring. The panther-woman's large almond-shaped eyes held him with the power of a siren's song.

Otto cuffed the side of Spike's head to break the daze.

"Helga's father thinks he can outsmart fate," Otto explained, as Spike turned to face forward. "Karl knows that one more girl will go missing this year. So he goes everywhere with his daughter. He never leaves her alone."

Spike nodded. "Hoping Helga won't get snatched if he's around."

"Every few years someone tries it." Otto sighed. "That's why we need Peak. You'll see."

Spike didn't have to see to imagine. A man could be overwhelmed by Peak's provocative charms. Being a vampire, he was less susceptible than a human would be. Besides, he loved Drusilla too much to ever be unfaithful.

Otto took the dirt road that skirted the village and stopped the car where a lane intersected the main route through town. The narrow road meandered through the valley countryside and down the mountain to a distant highway.

"They should be here soon, Peak," Otto said, as she opened the back door and stepped out.

"Don't worry, Otto." Peak closed the door and leaned against the rear fender. Dressed in a demure skirt, heavy shoes, and a business jacket, and with her black hair combed into a neat twist, she looked like a stranded lady in distress.

Spike, Otto, and Trevor slipped out of the car and into the darkness as Karl Lutze's truck rattled down the road. The farmer and his daughter had spent the afternoon selling vegetables in the village market square and were headed back to the farm.

When Peak stepped into the glare of the headlights and waved for the truck to stop, Karl hit the brakes.

The farmer spoke in German as he got out and strolled toward her.

"Excellent," Trevor whispered in Spike's ear. "He asked if she needs help."

Peak replied in German, and stared into the man's eyes, mesmerizing him before she finished speaking. He didn't notice that the tire in the Mercedes wasn't flat.

"Did she just call him 'pumpkin'?" Otto whispered, but started moving toward the truck before Trevor answered.

"Sometimes she calls them pumpernickel," Trevor told Spike. "Or petunia. They don't hear what she says. They are prisoners of the pheromones, deaf and blind to everything except Peak."

As they neared the truck, Spike pulled a cloth and a bottle from his pocket. He hesitated, feeling disturbed, but he couldn't say why. He had been uneasy since the last kidnapping foray, but there was no time to ponder it. He twisted the cap off the bottle.

Helga called to her as Peak enticed the farmer into the backseat of the Mercedes.

Otto ripped open the passenger door and pulled the startled girl out. Her fearful cry died in her throat when Spike covered her nose and mouth with the chloroform cloth. She collapsed in Otto's arms.

Spike studied the quarry in the dim glow of the truck's headlights. The girl was beautiful, like a china doll with pale, translucent skin, ringlets of dark brown hair, and red lips. Machida would be pleased.

When the car door opened and the farmer's body tumbled out, Spike couldn't hide his surprise. "What happened?"

"The cat kills her mates with the poisonous venom in her teeth and claws." Trevor chuckled. "They die instantly."

"That puts a damper on the tumble, doesn't it?" Spike shuddered.

"There must be no witnesses," Otto said as he lifted Helga.

Spike followed Otto to the car, but he left a measure of respect for Machida and his minions in the dirt. He had realized what troubled him the moment he put the cloth on the girl's face. There was nothing challenging or sporting about Otto and Trevor's methods. They were common criminals locked into an uninspired routine for a lazy reptilian monster that bribed others to hunt for him.

Disgusted—with himself and his companions— Spike forced a friendly attitude during the drive back up the mountain. Although Otto was a glorified flunky, the barbarian had treated Spike fairly and well. Spike wouldn't do anything to damage Otto's standing with his demon master. Whether Machida rewarded his efforts or not, Spike would leave Black Thorn Castle and Germany immediately after the demon's ritual feast.

The normally quiet and orderly castle routine was thrown into chaos on Machida's banquet day. Spike stayed in his room, plotting the safest course out of Europe through Switzerland, but it was impossible to ignore the unusual interaction of humans and demons outside his door. Slug moved up and down the stairways between the kitchen and the dungeon, digesting grit and moss that soiled the stone. Pond prowled every level, consuming uninvited pests.

The cook and maids had been sent away for the duration of the two days of preparation, ritual ceremony, and celebration. Klaus's wife, Ingrid, had recruited Otto and Trevor to work in the kitchen.

The von Hardt daughters, Ilse and Frieda, rushed about fussing over candles, robes, and other ritual accoutrements. Klaus's son, Dirk, and Frieda's husband, Lars Warner, guarded the three kidnapped girls, who were chained to the dungeon wall one level down.

Trevor had a knack for knowing everything that happened within the castle walls and had reported that Klaus was expanding his influence and power by offering the benefits of serving Machida to selected outsiders. The first nonfamily member, a person of importance Ingrid greatly wanted to impress, would be inducted before the demon's ritual feast tonight.

When Peak scratched at his door, Spike assumed she wanted a place to hide from the frantic activities. Cats, in his experience, despised disruptions and could not be forced in any endeavor to cooperate against their will. When he opened the door, the black panther leaped inside. Peak sat on her haunches, twitching her tail in agitation until he closed the door. Then she morphed into human form and covered herself with the blanket on Spike's bed.

"I don't mind if you stay here, Peak," Spike said, "but I'd rather be alone with the cat."

"You'll be leaving soon, vampire." Peak purred.

"I'm not going anywhere until after Machida stuffs himself with terrified teenagers," Spike said. He had told Otto his plans, thanking him for the honor of serving Machida and apologizing for an incurable wanderlust that compelled him to move on. He hoped Otto would put in a good word for him with Klaus regarding payment for kidnappings well done.

"Otto said you know of Hitler's demon hunters." A growl sounded deep in Peak's throat.

"I had a run-in with them a few months back." Spike frowned. "Why?"

"Klaus has a visitor," Peak hissed. "He wears silver and black and the death's head on his hat. Is he here for you?"

"The SS thinks I burned in the sun." Spike sat at his table, mulling the possible reasons von Hardt was entertaining an officer of the SS. "There's just the one man?"

"And a driver," Peak said. "He's outside with the car."

"Then chances are this man is here to pledge his life and all to Machida," Spike said. "I doubt there's anything to fear. He won't want anyone outside the castle to know he was here. Der Führer would execute an officer that swore allegiance to someone—or something—else."

"Otto said that Machida would protect us." Peak curled up on the bed. "But I do not want to encounter this man in the halls. If he liked me, I would have to kill him."

"Probably not a good plan." Spike sighed with relief when Peak morphed back into a panther and promptly fell asleep. He turned his attention back to the map. There wasn't a good escape route. To reach a port, he had to go through Mussolini's Italy or German-occupied France.

Without complaint, Spike donned the brown hooded monk's robes Otto had given him. Although it seemed unlikely Herr von Hardt's guest would remember him as the fried fugitive from Hamburg, Spike welcomed the anonymity the cowl provided. Even so, the von Hardt family's lack of imagination rankled him. Every demon-worshiping human cult Spike had encountered employed some form of chanting, candles, and monks' robes.

Since Peak had Machida's promise of protection and couldn't control the effects of her pheromones, Klaus had excused her from the ceremony.

Everyone else gathered in the dungeon torture chamber at midnight. Ingrid, Ilse, and Frieda stood with Lars and Dirk on one side of the chamber, with Spike, Otto, Trevor, and Pond—all robed with heads bowed, to avoid the stranger's curious stare—on the opposite side. Machida's female sacrifices occupied the space between them, manacled by chains bolted into the ceiling. Candles flickered in wall sconces, and metal devices designed to inflict pain reflected the light. A tunnel had been bored through the crumbling mortar wall into the side of the mountain. It led to Machida's lair.

Klaus von Hardt and the SS initiate stood in the center of the room. Klaus held a sword in one hand and pushed his hood off his head with the other. Naked to the waist with a hood over his head, the new man stood with his hands clasped behind his back. He didn't flinch when Klaus removed the hood and pressed the tip of the sword into his flesh.

Spike raised his eyes without lifting his head as Klaus began to chant the induction oath.

The German words faded into background noise as Spike focused on the SS officer's face. He had only seen it once before, from afar on a dark night, but the voice that repeated Machida's oath was too distinctive to forget. Machida's new disciple was Colonel Jürgen Koch, Hitler's demon hunter.

Spike lowered his eyes and stared at the floor.

The colonel finished his oath solemnly.

"In seinem Namen," the other humans repeated.

Dirk took his father's sword and shoved the blade into a pit of hot coals.

Klaus clasped Koch's shoulder, welcoming him into the fold. *"Sie sind jetzt mit uns."*

Ingrid walked over and slipped a brown robe over Koch's head.

"Danke." The colonel clicked his heels together with an abrupt bow. Then he joined the others of his species.

Spike wanted out of the room, out of the castle, and out of Germany, but his ceremonial obligations weren't over yet. Machida still had to be fed.

Ilse and Frieda lit more candles.

Klaus knelt and slipped off his robe, revealing diamond-shaped scars that had been burned into his chest, arms, and back. Dirk removed the heated sword from the coals and burned a new line on his father's back. When he was done, Ingrid placed a green robe onto Klaus's shoulders.

The teenage girls whimpered, too frightened or exhausted to scream.

Klaus walked to a stone altar and shook three

stones out of a leather pouch. He washed them with wine, picked up the sword, and held it point down in front of him. "Machida."

"*In seinem Namen,*" the others said.

"*Wir, die Sie dienen,*" Klaus continued.

Otto softly repeated the incantation in English for Spike. "We who serve you, we who receive all that you bestow, call upon you in this holy hour. We have no wealth . . ."

Neither do I, Spike thought. *No wealth and no patience for this prattle.* The lack of spontaneity and innovation in the ritual was annoying and offensive, an insult to the dark nobility of evil. Machida was a demonic disgrace, content with a monotonous ritual his followers had practiced unchanged for centuries, demanding nothing but a meager repast.

". . . no possession except what you give us," Otto went on. "We have no power, no place in the world except that which you give us."

Fools, Spike thought, wishing the sordid business was done so he could be on his way. No amount of wealth and power was worth his self-respect.

"Accept our offering, Dark Lord," Otto mumbled, "and bless us with your power."

"Machida!" Klaus intoned as he dropped each of the three stones onto the altar, before continuing to speak in German to the demon.

The reptilian demon exploded out of the tunnel, rising on his massive tail, his webbed arms outstretched to embrace the maiden offerings. Dark eyes glittered from sunken holes in a humanoid head covered with scales. He roared, revealing white teeth set in bloodred flesh.

Otto swayed as though in a trance, repeating the words he had heard every year for four hundred years. "For he shall rise from the depths, and we will tremble before him. He who is the source of all we inherit and all we possess. Machida."

The girls screamed. Spike was silent as humans and demons chanted the beast's name over and over again. Lars and Dirk freed the goat girl and dragged her toward the demon.

Spike blocked the sounds and smells of the voracious slaughter from his senses. He wasn't squeamish. He had engaged in melees of wanton murder many times, but Machida's followers had forfeited control of their own destinies, and that repulsed him.

When it was over, Spike tried to slip away. The floor was slick with blood, and the stagnant air was haunted by the whispered shrieks of all who had died within the dungeon walls. He almost didn't turn when Klaus called him back, speaking in halting English.

"Otto tells me you're leaving, Spike."

"I've seen enough here," Spike retorted, cloaking a snide response with innocuous words.

"Not everyone is content to stay in one place," Klaus said. "I respect that, but I also owe you for the work you've done."

Spike bit back a flippant comment when Klaus reached under his robe and pulled out an envelope.

"My driver will take you to Madrid tomorrow night." Klaus handed Spike the envelope. "New papers and enough money to take you wherever you want to go from there."

"Thank you." As Spike started up the stairs, Klaus called after him again. He paused to look down.

"Since you'll be in Madrid, you might want to check out the address in the envelope as well." Klaus smiled. "That is, if you're interested in a free virgin-blood party."

Atlantic Ocean
1943

Spike had gone to Madrid and the party. One minute he was asking why all the girls looked like Geobbels, and the next he was waking up on a bloody submarine at the bottom of the deep blue sea.

Spike swore as he forced his arms and legs to move faster in the cold water. Of course, what the Nazis wanted with demons was no longer a mystery. There had been official papers aboard the sub that spelled it all out. The Nazis were experimenting on vampires to "stimulate and control" their brains. Controlled vampires could be conscripted into a formidable, if not unbeatable, army. *As long as the ranks don't get caught in the rising sun,* Spike thought.

Angelus had ended up on the sub because the American government was engaged in similar demonic studies. A group called the Human Research Initiative had blackmailed Angelus into mounting a one-vampire rescue mission to get back the stolen German sub-

marine. Spike hadn't known that until he overheard
Angelus talking with Lawson, before Angelus bit the
mortally wounded man to save him.

Twenty-four Hours Earlier

Sitting in the captain's chair entertained Spike for sixty
seconds. No one in the crew jumped to get him a drink,
and Angelus had gone with Ensign Lawson. Curious,
Spike crept toward the forward compartment.

". . . apparently they're in the SS," Lawson said.

Angelus was quick to reply. "Spike's not in the SS.
He just likes wearing the jacket."

Too bad it isn't bloody Colonel Koch's jacket, Spike
thought. Klaus had betrayed him as a gesture of good
faith to his new pal in the SS. The colonel had been
waiting to nab him at the virgin-blood party in Madrid.

"Yeah, that doesn't help me understand why we're
working with him," Lawson pressed. "Or keeping him
alive for that matter."

"I've got him under control," Angelus shot back.

"That's not the point." Lawson's temper flared.
"He killed my captain, sir."

"We may be able to use them," Angelus argued.
"We don't have much of a crew left."

Sorry about that. Spike frowned, wondering what
he had to do to get a drink. Angelus wouldn't let him
kill anyone else until they reached land.

"I don't think we'll need them." Lawson wouldn't
give up.

Neither would Angelus. "They're extra hands."

"They're monsters," Lawson countered. "And I don't know why we're—"

Angelus cut him off. "You don't need to know why. We've got to bring this sub in. Those are our orders."

So that's how it is. Spike returned to the captain's chair to think. He didn't know why Angelus was working for the Americans or why he wanted to get the sub to the States. He didn't really care. Angelus had stood up for him against a Yank who wanted him dead.

Atlantic Ocean
1943

Spike crawled up the beach and rolled onto his back to stare at the stars. A few still sparkled in a dark sky slowly fading to gray. He had a few minutes before the killer sun rose, and there were several summer homes within sprinting distance.

He had things to think about. Riddles. Life was filled with too much irony for it to be accidental.

If the Americans hadn't captured the German sub, he'd be lying on some Nazi scientist's lab table with his head cut open. Then, although Angelus had been sent to save the Yanks from Spike and his vampire mates, Angelus had taken his side against the ensign.

So I owe Angelus one, Spike thought. *Two, actually.* His old friend and mentor had also saved him from the Human Research Initiative. He had no doubt about that. If Angelus hadn't put him off the boat, the superscience folk would have grabbed him the instant he stepped off the deck. He'd rather swim a lagoon full of man-eating sharks than tangle with the toggle-and-circuit crowd on either side of the Atlantic.

If Angelus was smart, he'd jump ship too—before it reached port.

Spike staggered to his feet and headed for the nearest bungalow. He was anxious to see Dru, but he couldn't shake a sense of shared destiny with Angelus. Was that it? The ironic reason that explained the inexplicable? Spike didn't know, but one thing was clear: No matter how long he and Angelus were separated, they were irrevocably bound by the lineage of blood that had made them.

Chapter Nine

A dozen questions swirled in Spike's mind as he headed back to the factory from the induction ceremony at Delta Zeta Kappa. When had Machida moved from Bavaria to Southern California? Perhaps, since Klaus von Hardt was a Nazi sympathizer, he had been forced to abandon Black Thorn Castle when the Allies arrived. Was Tom Warner, the fraternity man named on the delivery receipt, a descendant of Frieda and Lars Warner? Had Otto and the other castle demons survived, or ended up in a Nazi lab? He wondered, but the past was a matter of curiosity, and irrelevant. The present was critical.

Dru would have to accept a young college man posing as a monk as a substitute for the Slayer's mom.

Spike had too much on his mind to care if she destroyed all her dolls or stopped talking to him for a day or two. Dru would eat whomever he brought home, or go hungry.

"Where is everybody?" Spike strode through the factory toward the Anointed One's overturned metal tub. The minions were usually lounging about the large room, playing poker for cockroaches, and arm wrestling, among other mindless diversions. It was long after sundown, and the room was empty.

Lucius scurried down the metal stairs from the upper floor. "Did you want something, Spike?"

"Yeah, I've got an announcement." Annoyed, Spike glanced up the stairs. "Are they up there?"

"Everyone except Dorian and Garbo," Lucius said. "They left at sunset to search for the book."

"I'm glad to hear they're taking that job seriously." Spike nodded, pleased. "But I have something to tell the others."

"Maybe I should deliver a message," Lucius suggested with a sheepish shrug. "After what happened to Hank, everyone's freaked."

"Whatever." Spike wasn't going to coddle the crew. He needed all his coddling energies to placate Dru. "Just get them down here before I get back. Ten minutes. Everyone eats tonight."

Spike sent Lucius away without disclosing the details. The underlings would hunt, but with restrictions. He didn't want to kill anyone else because they couldn't wait five minutes and jumped the gun.

"Where is she?" Dru looked up from Miss Martha's

funeral basket when Spike walked in. "I've been rehears-ing a lit'le speech about her treacherous Slayer spawn and how you're going to kill her."

"The Slayer's mum is off the menu, Dru," Spike said. There was no point making excuses or fudging the facts. Dru always knew when he was lying. That was the downside of her erratic prescience.

"A cart is no good without a pony." Dru's eyes darkened with rage. "Did Miss Martha die for nothing?"

"No, Dru," Spike said. "She died because you don't need her anymore."

Dru's brow furrowed as she grasped the meaning of his words. "I'll be better soon. Then I won't need the tonic."

"Very soon, and then you'll be too busy to bother with dolls." Spike put his arms around her. He was determined to restore her physical health, but there wasn't a miracle cure for the vagaries of her deranged mind. "Dorian and Garbo are out now, searching for the book with the recipe to make you right."

"Are you going to spoil the nasty boys' party?" Dru asked, changing the subject as she pressed against him.

Spike suspected it was a trick question and groped for the right answer. "Only so I can steal a snake demon's tidbit girls for you, pet."

"Girls are nice," Dru said. "When I'm better, will I be all sugar and spice, like gumdrops?"

Sunnydale
September 2002

". . . sugar and spice and everything . . ." *Warren* faltered, his voice steeped in loathing for girls. ". . . useless unless you're bacon."

The apparition was making less sense than Dru, Spike realized. He had usually been able to figure out what Drusilla meant. The Other apparently had a problem with women, and *Warren*—who had used spells and built robots to get a date—was the ideal vehicle for Its anger.

"I'm more than that," *Warren* said, seething with indignation. "More than flesh . . ."

The flesh is not what burns, Spike thought. His mind burned with memories of things that never were and couldn't be because of a nibble on his neck and the taste of blood. He had the spark now, but it didn't fit right, and he would never have the girl because of flesh . . . and blood.

". . . more than blood," *Glory* continued where *Warren* left off. "I am—you know, I honestly don't think there's a human word fabulous enough for me."

Even in his delirium, Spike could think of a few. *Vile, malevolent, fiendish, conceited, reprehensible, depraved . . .*

"Oh, my name will be on everyone's lips, assuming their lips haven't been torn off." *Glory* smiled. "But not just yet."

But soon, Spike thought. Something was coming,

something big and ugly that blond curls and red silk couldn't disguise, something from beneath to end it all. This time he knew, expected it. Not the punch line to a cruel joke, not blindsided—

Sunnydale
October 1997

The minions made no sound as they climbed over the cemetery wall. Spike stood on the curved tree trunk, watching as each one vanished into the dark woods. Letting them hunt the Delta Zeta Kappa party would solve two problems: After the hungry vampires were fed, they'd stop moping, complaining, and getting on his nerves. And the fraternity with its resident demon would take the blame for the dead bodies the police found on the grounds.

Machida had changed location, but Spike was certain that no aspect of the reptile's tedious MO had changed. The snake still bribed ambitious men to kidnap girls, chant his praises, and mutilate themselves with white-hot swords. In return for playing medieval dress-up and performing his inane ritual, Machida's followers enjoyed excessive wealth and success. The pattern had been repeated without deviation for centuries. No one knew what would happen if Machida missed a meal.

But we'll find out tonight, Spike thought with a smug smile. He'd kill the parasite Machida for fun. Certainly the snake's paltry contributions to the accumulated works of evildoers wouldn't be missed. More important, the bank accounts, businesses, and reputations of the demon's disciples and their heirs would go down the sodding drain. *Easy come, easy go,* Spike thought, snagging Lucius as he dropped to the ground.

"Everyone hunts from the woods along the drive and parking area," Spike told his lieutenant. "Any party people catch a glimpse of a vampire, and someone gets a stake for dessert."

"Nobody will see us," Lucius assured him.

"Good. This gala will probably go on a couple more hours, plenty of time for the crew to feed," Spike said. "Then I want everyone gone, except you and Chain. I'll be waiting in the trees out front."

"I'd rather bring Gator," Lucius said. "He moves faster and doesn't ask questions."

"Your call." Spike had no intention of disappointing Dru twice in one night. He'd needed reliable help to take the three girls from their captors and transport them back to the factory. "We're going to bust some monk-boy chops and steal a demon's dinner."

After Lucius ran into the woods, Spike slipped into stealth mode—not invisible, but unnoticed—as he scouted the house. He had a clear view of the party rooms through several open windows. Loud music blared from multiple speakers mounted inside and out. The hacienda was packed, and the overflow spilled out onto the lawns. Young men and women danced and flirted with drinks in hand. A few odd men out were being rude and obnoxious, a universal behavior when money, position, and birthright gave lesser men power over those who were common-born, smarter, and better looking. He'd be doing the whole bloody world a favor when he killed the golden goose that supported these privileged losers.

"Remember your manners." A man in a dark blazer admonished two men who were ogling women and making crude comments.

One of the jerks nudged the other. "That's Tom Warner, the top gun around here. Better do what he says."

He even looks like Lars, Spike thought as Tom walked into the next room. That didn't prove the young man was descended from Frieda and Lars, but it was a stretch to think the presence of Machida and the family resemblance was a coincidence.

Since the fraternity wouldn't begin the ritual to call Machida until the party was over, Spike had time to kill. He wandered over to the driveway to check on the minions.

Cars were parked bumper to bumper on both sides of the wide drive on the west side of the hacienda. The area under the arched portico spanning the road was brightly lit. The street lamps along the drive were spaced too far apart, and circles of light were separated by stretches of darkness. Spike hid in the shadows near the house and scanned for vampire activity.

A red corvette whipped up the drive and parked in front of the portico support. A tall, well-dressed young man in slacks and a blazer got out. The instant he slammed the car door closed, he disappeared. No one else noticed the sounds Spike's enhanced hearing picked up: the muffled boy trying to scream as his captor dragged him into the trees.

Satisfied that his fearful followers were obeying his orders and keeping a low profile, Spike edged out of the shrubs to find a more private spot to have a smoke. The screech of tires caught his attention, and he flinched when a red sedan plowed into the back of a parked convertible. He realized the gods of irony were toying with him when he saw Cordelia Chase behind the wheel and the Slayer in the passenger seat.

Looking into college for a school project, huh? Spike doubted that Joyce had envisioned a fraternity party when Buffy made her excuses on the phone.

The Slayer's rebellious streak was an intriguing trait Spike would take into account when he moved against her, but that wouldn't be tonight. He wasn't about to challenge the Slayer with the henchmen running about in a feeding frenzy, Dru craving a special treat, a hundred mortal witnesses, and the party hosts preparing for their annual sacrifice to a gigantic snake. He was good, but he wasn't a fool. Killing the Slayer required his total attention.

"Why do they park so darn close to you?" Cordelia checked her hair in the rearview mirror, either oblivious or unconcerned about the damage she had done to a stranger's car. "Are you ready for this?"

"I don't know." Buffy looked as enthusiastic as a fire sprite walking a pirate's plank. "Maybe this wasn't a good idea."

"Me too," Cordelia said. "Let's go."

Oblivious, Spike thought as Cordelia unbuckled and got out of the car. The self-centered, bossy shrew he had observed at The Bronze masquerade was the real Cordelia Chase. Her only redeeming quality was that she treated Buffy the same as she did everyone else—like an idiot. That entitled her to a temporary, but not indefinite, stay of execution. He despised stuck-up socialites. If he hadn't promised to bring Dru the girls designated for Machida's feast, this would be Cordelia's farewell fling.

Buffy seemed so uncertain and uncomfortable, Spike was sure she had come to party and not to slay. The short black dress supported that conclusion. Her social life usually included Willow the Winsome, Xander the Clueless, and Angel, the brooding dead man, so she was out of her element among the rich and demented. She would have been rock-hard sure of herself going into a fight. By the look of it, she didn't know the fraternity had a demon mascot in the basement.

You'd better be here to have a good time, Slayer. This is my turf tonight, Spike thought as he shadowed the girls.

Spike stayed outside when Buffy and Cordelia entered the crowded house. In places such as The Bronze he could fade into the background like a chameleon. He would stand out like blood on snow at Delta Zeta Kappa. The frat brothers knew everyone in their ranks and on their guest list. Instead, he moved from window to window, tracking Buffy and eavesdropping. There was no such thing as too much information when prepping for a death match with a slayer.

"You know what's so cool about college?" Cordelia asked Buffy. They stood alone in a doorway, trying to look as though they belonged. "The diversity. You've got all the rich people, and all the other people. Richard!"

"Welcome, ladies." A young man in a sports coat walked up and handed each girl a drink.

"Thank you," Cordelia said, smiling brightly.

"Oh, is there alcohol in this?" Buffy asked.

"Just a smidge," Richard assured her.

Oh, come on! Spike groaned inwardly. He could understand why Cordelia would be smitten into mental numbness by handsome money, but the Slayer should be too smart to fall for the smooth older-man routine. *No, wait,* he reminded himself. Buffy was smitten with the ultimate older man—Angel, a vampire who had scared her off with grim happily-never-afters. She was partying to forget him.

"Come on, Buffy," Cordelia said. "It's just a smidge."

"I'll just—" Buffy put the glass down.

"I understand." Richard smiled. "When I was your age, I wasn't into grown-up things either."

Spike's eyes narrowed. The snide remark pegged Richard as a condescending creep. He and Cordelia deserved each other.

A thrashing in the bushes drew Spike away. He assumed one of the minions had gone off course and was hunting too close to the house. He hurried toward the sound and turned the corner just as Buffy's lanky friend, Xander, fell through the open window he had used to get into the house.

"He's hopeless," Spike mumbled, finding a place to watch the continuing saga of the Slayer's hapless sidekick. The boy had stuck his neck out for Angel, fallen for a mummy, and now he was crashing a frat party in a demon's lair. He should kill Xander just to put him out of his bumbling misery.

Xander grabbed a drink off a tray carried by a Delta Zeta Kappa pledge wearing a bib and a diaper. He sauntered through the party trying to look cool, but his slicked-back hair, khaki pants, and red polo shirt betrayed him, as if shouting, "This guy doesn't belong here!"

Cordelia was gone, but Buffy was still standing in the same spot, alone with her untouched drink, the winner of the night's most pathetic wallflower award.

Good show on not falling for the pickup line, Slayer, but dull. Spike went to follow Xander for some comic relief to help pass the time while he waited for the main event.

Xander was now in the company of two women, a blonde and a brunette. They were alive, but too embarrassed or disbelieving to speak when he suddenly used hors d'oeuvres to mimic a Japanese movie monster.

"Godzilla attacking downtown Tokyo!" Xander roared. "Argh! Argh!"

As Xander and his women wandered off, a frat boy in a blue shirt and tie joined Richard in a nearby doorway. "Who's this dork?"

"Never seen him before in my life," Richard said.

"We've got us a crasher." A third man with short hair peered over Richard's shoulder.

Spike frowned as the three frat brats walked over to Xander and his lady friends. The college men were predators on the prowl, and Xander was their unwary prey.

"So, have either of you seen a pair of girls here?" Xander asked the women. "One's about . . . so high?"

Then he noticed the men behind him. "Hey, guys."

"New pledge!" The man in the blue shirt yelled.

"New pledge!" The man with short hair repeated.

Other men in the room took up the call as Richard's two friends dragged Xander away. A crowd gathered around as they pulled Xander's shirt and trousers off and forced him to don a woman's skirt and bra.

Spike turned away. He didn't want to witness the boy's humiliation. He couldn't kill him now either. Xander shouldn't die the same night the snobs and elitists demeaned him, flaunting their folderol and slinging abusive remarks as though he didn't have feelings. Xander had friends, and wasn't in need of saving as Dru had saved Spike.

London
1880

The poems did not come easily. William stared at the papers in his lap, barely hearing the soft strains of music and chatter around him. He had tried ever so hard to come up with a word that rhymed with "gleaming" and had failed utterly.

". . . luminous. No, no, no." He scratched it out. "You're radiant . . . better."

"Care for an hors d'oeuvre, sir?" a waiter asked, holding out a tray.

William took his pen out of his mouth to speak. "Oh, ah—quickly. I'm the very spirit of vexation. What's another word for gleaming?"

The waiter lifted his chin, perplexed.

"It's a perfectly perfect word as words go," William explained. "But the bother is nothing rhymes, you see."

The man smiled and moved on.

William stopped fretting when Cecily walked down the stairs. In her white gown with lavender collar and matching flounces, and her hair gathered in curls atop her head, she was as beautiful as he remembered in his dreams and strove to capture with his words.

"Cecily . . ." Just saying her name inspired him. The elusive word William had been searching for jumped into his head, and he hastened to write it down. When he was done, he rose to join Cecily's group of friends.

"I merely point out that it's something of a mystery, and the police should keep an open mind," Cecily's lady friend said. William could never remember the woman's name.

"Ah, William," a gentleman in a green jacket said. "Favor us with your opinion. What do you make of this rash of disappearances sweeping through our town? Animals or thieves?"

"I prefer not to think of such dark, ugly business at all," William said, rather pompously. "That's what the police are for." He chanced a glance at Cecily and noted how it flustered her. She lowered her eyes, and he took the opportunity to assure her that he was not a brute but had the gentle sensibilities of an artist. "I prefer to place my energies into creating things of beauty."

"I see. Well, don't withhold, William." The gentleman in green snatched Cecily's poem from his hand.

The lady in red urged the man on. "Rescue us from a dreary topic."

"Careful." William reached for the paper. The man warned him off with a hard look, but he persisted. The words had been penned for Cecily, no one else. "The inks are still wet. Please, it's not finished."

"Don't be shy." The man began to recite. "'My heart expands, 'tis grown a bulge in it, inspired by your beauty, effulgent.'"

William watched Cecily, his heart swelling when she seemed overwhelmed by his words.

"Effulgent?" The man chuckled, as did the lady in the red gown. When everyone nearby started laughing, Cecily fled.

William grabbed the poem and went after her.

"And that's actually one of his better compositions," another man observed.

"Haven't you heard?" Cecily's lady friend asked. "They call him William the Bloody because of his bloody awful poetry."

"It suits him," the man in green agreed. "I'd rather have a railroad spike through my head than listen to that awful stuff."

William ignored the taunts. Most of the people at the soiree were too insulated by their wealth and prestige to appreciate independent effort and artistry. Cecily was from a family of means and position too, but she was different. He approached her quietly, touched by her concern for him.

"Cecily?"

She turned suddenly, startled to see him. "Oh, leave me alone."

"Oh, they're vulgarians." William sat on the sofa beside her. "They're not like you and I."

"You and I?" Cecily dropped her fan in her lap, as though the thought of them together had just occurred to her. "I'm going to ask you a very personal question. And I demand an honest answer. Do you understand?"

William's throat constricted. He had hardly dared hope Cecily might have feelings for him. His love for her buoyed his flagging spirits and carried him through days consumed with worry for his sick mother. How much easier everything would be with the woman he loved at his side, sharing the joys and sorrows of life.

He barely managed to murmur, "Yes."

"Your poems—" Cecily hesitated. "They're not written about me, are they?"

"They're about how I feel," William answered.

"Yes, but are they about me?" Cecily pressed.

She had asked him to be honest. He couldn't deny her that trust. "Every syllable."

"Oh, God!" Cecily looked away, overcome, and she dropped her head in her hand and began whimpering.

"Oh, I know—it's sudden." William had lulled himself to sleep many nights rehearsing the right words to say, but now that the moment had come, they were lost to him. "And, and, please—if they're no good, they're only words, but—"

She looked distraught, and he wanted to comfort her.

"—the feeling behind them. I love you, Cecily."

"Please, stop." Cecily turned away.

"I—I know I'm a bad poet," William confessed, "but I'm a good man. All I ask is that . . . is that you try to see me—"

"I do see you," Cecily said. "That's the problem. You're nothing to me, William." She stood up. "You're beneath me."

Sunnydale
September 2002

"That's all right, though," *Glory* said.

Actually, no, it isn't all right. Spike frowned at the storeroom floor. *Why isn't it?* He tried to fight the force that didn't want him to think or question everything he had blindly accepted as truth.

Perceptions changed with time and experience. A sentient existence was influenced and shaped by events. Understanding expanded as knowledge was gained.

What he thought he knew wasn't necessarily what was so.

A revelation darted back and forth under the surface of Spike's conscious mind, looking for a way through the barrier that shielded his awareness. His memories had been fixed for so long, frozen and resistant to new interpretations.

He had been devastated because Cecily had thought him unworthy of even the most casual concern. She couldn't see him for the man he had been because she couldn't be bothered to look.

The barrier cracked, and a glimmer of realization shone through the vengeful voices and fog.

Why hadn't he seen Cecily for who *she* really was before she had crushed his fragile heart?

It had never occurred to Spike to ask, perhaps because he wouldn't have known the answer. He did now, and he could no longer hide from a truth that was a balm and a thorn.

He had believed winning Cecily's affections would end the ridicule and win the respect of his peers. That had been folly, but not the worst of it. On another, deeper level, he had thought Cecily's love would validate his sense of self and dispel his uncertainties about his manliness. How dreadfully wrong he had been. Cecily had preferred the company of shallow bores to the love of a poet.

Glory transformed into *Adam*. "I can be patient. Everything is well within parameters. She's exactly where I want her to be."

That's what Spike had thought once.

Sunnydale
October 1997

The hazing of Xander by the men of Delta Zeta Kappa was a mean and meaningless exercise of power. They tormented him because they could, knowing no one would dare try to stop them. And no one did.

That's the way of the world, Spike thought as he walked away from the spectacle. Survival of the fittest, the strongest prevail—except when the weak had a champion, like he was for Dru and the Slayer was for Xander. Except that she was not rushing to his rescue.

Spike spotted Buffy on the veranda, apparently deaf and blind to her friend's predicament. She was alone, holding her arms as though chilled. Her forlorn expression was more suited to the tragic figures of great literature than a supergirl who could wipe the floor with the Delta Zeta Kappas.

Hugging the stucco wall, Spike edged closer as Buffy stooped to pick up a shard of broken glass, and then looked up at the second-floor window. She frowned, her suspicious gaze sweeping the expansive lawn as she stood up. If she didn't already know, how long would it take her to figure out that the fraternity had a resident demon?

"You okay?" Tom Warner walked toward her.

Machida's top gun meets the Slayer, Spike thought, annoyed. Irony was working overtime.

Startled, Buffy dropped the piece of glass. It was a guilty reaction, but Tom didn't seem to notice. "Yeah. I was just thinking."

Richard strolled out to join them, carrying three drinks. "To my Argentinean junk bonds that just matured into double digits." He handed Buffy and his friend each a glass.

"To maturity," Tom said.

"What the hell. I'm tired of being mature." Buffy chugged the drink.

Richard and Tom exchanged a glance that could only be read as a victory gloat.

Was Tom putting serious moves on his slayer? Spike bristled. The intensity of the jealous surge surprised him, but he was the alpha hunter and Buffy was the championship trophy prey. He didn't like the idea of anyone tarnishing the grand prize. Still, it was petty to begrudge the Slayer a little romance in the short time she had left. Angel wouldn't even take her out for coffee.

Bored with the frat scene, Spike slipped into the woods to warn the minions that the dinner hour was almost over. People were starting to leave, and he wanted to attack the instant the monk-boys started Machida's ceremony.

Spike sat in the crook made by a large tree trunk and a heavy branch, watching the driveway and house. Most of the guests had gone, and the bad boys of Delta Zeta Kappa were booting the stragglers. He hadn't seen Buffy or Cordelia leave, but the lecherous Richard and Tom were probably enjoying a lingering good-night kiss. They were still boys despite their gruesome hobby. He looked toward the veranda and the sound of laughter.

Xander stumbled out the door, shoved by the rude man in the tie. He still wore the skirt and a stuffed bra with the addition of smudged lipstick and a long blond wig.

"Party's over, jerkwater." The man with the short hair threw Xander his bundled clothes.

"Wait!" Xander said. "A friend of mine was here."

That made Spike sit up and take notice. The only friend of Xander's at the party was Buffy. Despite his obvious embarrassment, he was asking about her instead of running as fast and far away as possible.

"You know, in that light,"—the man in the tie hitched up his pants—"with that wig on and all . . . you're still butt ugly!"

Both men laughed and slammed the door in Xander's face.

Xander pulled the wig off and removed the gigantic bra. He dropped them on the porch and left.

"Spike!" Lucius stood at the base of the tree, whispering. Spike had sent him and Gator to watch the window by the basement door. If one of Machida's dinner dates made a break for it, they had orders to grab her.

"Where's Gator?" Spike hissed back.

"He's still watching the window," Lucius said. "The monk-boys just dragged two girls into the basement."

"Just now?" Spike arched an eyebrow. That was cutting it close. Otto wouldn't have put off a kidnapping until the last minute, but then the big barbarian hadn't been able to throw a party to lure his victims. "What did they look like?"

"A blonde in black and a brunette in green," Lucius explained. "Drugged, I think. They weren't very steady on their feet."

So they did have designs on my slayer, Spike thought, steamed. Drugging Buffy's drink was the only way a bunch of milquetoast college boys could have nabbed her. They wanted Buffy for demon food, not fooling around, and probably didn't know they had captured an empowered legendary hero. With Cordelia and the runaway from the cemetery, the monk-boys had three.

Spike jumped down from his perch. "Go back to Gator and keep an eye on that window. If anyone uses it to leave, capture but don't kill."

Spike's mind raced as Lucius zigzagged through the trees. He hadn't wanted to fight the Slayer with distractions, but the minions were gone, and if the monk-boys had managed to manacle Buffy before she was fully conscious, he'd be a fool to pass up the opportunity.

With Lucius and Gator along to mangle the frat boys, Spike could get some overdue revenge. Klaus von Hardt had betrayed him to Colonel Koch of the SS, but Machida could have prevented the treachery. Spike had served the reptile and earned the protection the demon snake had chosen to withhold. Since Klaus was long dead, Machida and Tom, Lars Warner's descendant, could settle the score.

Once Machida was skewer meat, he'd free Cordelia and kill her while the chained Slayer watched. Dru would just have to be happy with the third girl and a monk-boy. Then—what? Spike frowned as he stepped out of the trees. Killing a slayer who had been captured and chained by mortal snake worshippers wouldn't exactly enhance his reputation as a legendary evil.

Hearing footsteps on gravel, Spike ducked back under cover. Xander was walking down the drive, still wearing the skirt, carrying his regular clothes, and talking to himself.

"One day I'll have money, prestige, power," Xander said.

If you're lucky, which you're not. Spike sighed. Xander was a magnet for trouble—demonic and human. If something was looking for someone to mess with, it would find Xander. Money, prestige, and power weren't factors in the Xander equation.

"And on that day, they'll still have more," Xander concluded.

Not if their source is dead, Spike thought. When Xander suddenly headed back toward the house, Spike ran into the woods that bordered the front lawn. He paused when he heard the sputtering sound of an old car coming up the drive.

Rupert Giles parked the dilapidated Citroen and turned off the ignition. Before the engine stopped rumbling, the librarian, Willow, and Angel got out and moved through the trees with the vampire in the lead. Spike silently faded back as they filed past his position.

"Looks like everyone's gone," Willow said.

Everyone but me, and who invited you? Spike scowled as the trio lined up to survey the house. A twig snapped as a robed figure came up behind them.

"Hey!" Angel whirled to face the intruder. Willow's and Giles's reaction time lagged a second.

"Hey! What are you guys doing here?" Xander asked.

Having a bloody meeting of Slayer friends in the soddin' woods! Spike tightened his jaw, trying to keep a lid on his explosive frustration.

"A bunch of girls are missing," Willow explained. "The Zeta Kappas may be involved. And Buffy." She frowned, puzzled. "Are you wearing makeup?"

"No." Xander wiped lipstick off his mouth. "I think Buffy's still inside somewhere with Cordelia. Their car's still here."

"Why are you wearing that?" Giles pointed to the robe.

"I found it in their trash," Xander explained. "I saw them through the window. They were wearing robes and went down into the basement. I was gonna use it to sneak in."

"They may be involved in some kind of ritual," Giles said.

"With the missing girls," Willow added.

Angel vamped out and growled. "With Buffy."

"Okay," Xander said, "that is the guy you want to party with."

Spike threw up his hands as the four ran across the lawn toward the house. With the Slayer's misfit gang in the mix, the odds had gone against him. The three humans weren't a problem, but there was no reason to believe Angel's combat skills had diminished with the return of his soul. Defending a girl he cared about, even if he wouldn't admit it, would just make him stronger.

To avoid being seen, Spike ran through the woods for several yards before he turned toward the house to retrieve Gator and Lucius. The snake demon wouldn't die at his hands, but it would die tonight. Machida didn't stand a chance against the Slayer and the Sunnydale Do-in-a-demon-a-day Club.

Chapter Ten

Sunnydale
September 2002

"**A**nd so are you, Hostile Seventeen." *Adam* towered over Spike, skin and scales glistening in the dim storeroom light. "You're right where you belong."

No, that's the problem, Spike realized. *That's always been the problem.*

He focused on the feel of the rough cloth under his fingers, the pit mark in the floor, the dank smell of moisture and cement, but the army of facts kept coming, relentlessly. Bits and pieces of memory and knowledge chiseled chunks from the psychological barrier he had built to keep them out.

Truth had gotten back in with his soul, and it wouldn't be denied. Not anymore.

mind He had never belonged anywhere, had never been accepted.

William's presence among Cecily's friends had been tolerated—barely. Every social circle seemed to need someone to belittle, a court jester that would bear the insults and abuse without complaint. He had unwittingly filled that role, but was more pathetic for not having known it. Cecily had reviled him for this blind denial, for having dared sully her with the mere mention of his love.

Darla and Angelus had honored the blood lineage that bound him to them through Dru, but mostly they had put up with him and his reckless antics to please their addled daughter-granddaughter. Dru had loved him—until he formed a temporary alliance with the Slayer to keep Angelus from awakening Acathla and destroying the vampire food supply along with the world. When he drove away from Sunnydale with Dru, he had left his heart behind with Buffy. Dru knew it long before he did, and had finally sent him packing.

Each revelation hammered another chisel of hard, cold fact into the wall. Truth seeped into and split the cracks, exposing reality. Delusion and denial leaked out.

The Slayer's mismatched circle of friends had feared him and despised him. They had given Anya, an ex-vengeance demon with a long resume of evil accomplishments, a chance to prove she had changed. After the Initiative wired his brain for pain, the Scooby Gang had given him haven in a bathtub and a basement apartment, but only because they knew the bloody chip was controlling his vicious nature. When it became apparent he could hurt and kill evil, they had let him fight for good. Still, Giles and Xander had remained skeptical of his motives, and wary. Willow and Dawn had accepted him—but eventually he lost them too.

Buffy had never trusted him.

Spike stared at the floor, drowning in the flood of realization and remorse that swept brick and mortar away.

He loved the Slayer with a wild, dangerous, and consuming passion. Buffy thought it would flare and grow cold, but she was wrong. True love burned forever, as hot as a soul in a bad man. . . .

The Mayor replaced *Adam* as It squatted beside Spike. "So what did you think? You'd get your soul back and everything would be jim-dandy?"

Spike had hoped just that, but it was the absurd wish of a man muddled by love and desperation. The spark was an agony that seared every thought with guilt and regret. The pain was more excruciating than the punishment imposed by the chip, and no penance could erase or ease it.

"A soul is slipperier than a greased weasel." *The Mayor* laughed. "Why do you think I sold mine? Well, you'd probably thought you'd be your own man. I respect that, but—"

Sunnydale
October 1997

Spike sat in an upholstered chair in front of the TV with his feet propped on the end of the bed. The set was tuned to a trivia game show, but he wasn't paying attention. It was hard to hear over Dru's lecture to her dolls.

"This is what happens when mummy gets upset." Dru held out a small decorative urn as though the dolls could see. Miss Martha's ashes were inside the brass jar, stuffed into a velvet bag and tied with her green ribbon gag. "Bashed and burned, my darlings."

Spike glanced at her but didn't interrupt. He didn't want to trigger another bout of irrational raving. She had been depressed and angry for three weeks, since he had returned from the Delta Zeta Kappa party. Instead of Machida's maidens, he had brought her the obnoxious man in the tie who had harassed Xander.

Spike smiled, thinking back. He had reached the hacienda window where Gator and Lucius were waiting just before Buffy's intrepid assault force burst through the front door. What the Slayer's friends lacked in expertise, they made up for in fervor. He had witnessed a few of their best moves despite the fluttering curtain obstructing the view.

Xander had ridden the back of the tie guy, slugging him repeatedly. "That's for the wig!" *Bam!* "That's for the bra!" *Bam!* Giles had, surprisingly, decked one boy with a single backhand, and Angel had taken care of the rest. Willow had kept her wits about her and didn't wilt in the face of danger. When the four friends rushed into the basement to save Buffy, Spike had leaped through the window and captured Dru's dinner.

Seeing Buffy's minions in action was a gift of fate, Spike thought as he folded last Sunday's edition of the

Sunnydale Press and tossed it on the bed. He would not, as he had previously been inclined, underestimate the Slayer's pals in a fight. The three girls had been rescued, and a murderous college cult had been uncovered and broken up. The Sunnydale justice system moved faster than other courts, and all the men involved had been sentenced to consecutive life sentences.

Although there had been no mention of the giant snake in the newspaper, Spike assumed Machida was dead. Bones of missing girls had been found in a huge cavern beneath the frat house, some dating back fifty years. That timing supported his theory, that Lars Warner had brought Machida to California after World War II and introduced him to the boys of Delta Zeta Kappa. Several global enterprises, whose chairmen and founders had been members of the fraternity, were experiencing falling profits, IRS raids, and boardroom suicides.

"Miss Edith hears rumblings." Dru clutched the doll and turned toward Spike. "Grumble rumbles under the ground, all shaking and making the killer disappear." She closed her eyes and trembled. "Making you disappear, Spike. The bees buzzing all around, singing of smoke and fire."

Spike stood up to calm her before she lost control. "I can handle any fire that isn't solar, luv. You know that."

Dru swayed, caught in a powerful trance. "Cataclysm with the ugly little beasties screaming to get out, get out, but the sun melts the dark—" Her eyes popped open. She dropped Miss Edith and flailed at him with her fists.

"Easy, Dru—" Spike tried to catch her hands, but she had mustered a measure of strength and wrenched free. "Stop it, Dru—"

"Kill her, Spike." Dru pounded his chest, but the blows weakened quickly and stopped. "You've got to kill the Slayer before she poisons you."

"And how would she do that?" Spike asked gently, guiding her to the bed as she started to collapse. There was a poison called "killer of the dead," which could only be cured by the blood of a slayer, but he doubted Drusilla or Buffy knew of it. He had become a student of vampire vulnerabilities in his quest to find a cure for her ailment. "I'm a vampire."

"Foul, stinky mush all rotted inside." Dru grabbed a fistful of his shirt as she fell back on the pillows. "Kill her now, Spike.

"First chance I get," Spike said, pulling the quilt up under Dru's chin. Dru's outburst had put an unnecessary strain on her fragile constitution. He had postponed the inevitable slayer confrontation to concentrate on getting Dru well, but he had recently reassessed that decision.

The *du Lac Manuscript* was taking longer to find than he had anticipated. Dorian and Garbo couldn't enter the librarian's apartment to search without an invitation, and Giles hardly ever left the high school library, which limited the hours the two vampires could search. And now Dru's troublesome visions about the Slayer were eroding her remaining strength.

He couldn't afford to wait.

On his way out, Spike glanced in the birdcage and swore under his breath. The water and seed cups were empty. The new raven cowered against the bars as he refilled them. Dru had pouted for days after the first bird died of starvation. He had wasted precious research time catching another, but it wasn't going to last long if Dru couldn't remember to feed it.

Spike picked up the doll Drusilla had dropped and put it back with the others. "Miss Edith, remind her to feed the damn bird."

Jacob was waiting for him in the main room. When Spike decided to modernize his surveillance techniques, he had found an expert in video systems and turned him into a vampire. Then he had stolen the necessary equipment from Jacob's ex-employer. Jacob was proving to be a valuable asset. He had videotaped Buffy fighting another new minion the night before and had spent the day installing monitor screens and playback machines in the factory.

"Are we set up yet, Jacob?" Spike asked.

"Ready to roll, Spike." Jacob smiled nervously.

"Is something wrong?" Spike eyed him curiously. He had assured the electronics expert that he was not expendable, but Jacob was still shaken by the death of the other new minion on the slayer assignment.

"No," Jacob said quickly. "I'm pretty sure I got it all."

"Well, let's see it, then." Spike looked up at the screen suspended from the ceiling as Jacob clicked the remote.

The opening shot showed a large wagon decked

out with scarecrows, jack-o'-lanterns, colored corn, and strings of pumpkin lights. A tall, thin vampire stepped out from behind a row of trees, grabbed the Slayer from behind, and heaved her toward a display under the POP'S PUMPKIN PATCH sign. She landed on a lighted jack-o'-lantern, squashing it.

"Excellent." Spike nodded as the vampire toppled some hay bales and roared to menace the downed Slayer. He glanced at Jacob. "What was his name again?"

"Bobby." Jacob hit pause, then reversed the tape a few frames.

Spike waved to continue, and the tape resumed as the Slayer picked up a gourd. She heaved it at Bobby, hitting him in the forehead. He staggered, and then staggered again when a pumpkin smashed into his face. Buffy was on her feet before Bobby regained his balance. She threw a stake. He blocked it with a scarecrow.

"Nice move," Spike said, nodding.

Bobby whirled to increase momentum for a karate kick, but Buffy ducked. He tried to kick again, but she fended it off with a series of punches. They traded several blows until she grabbed his coat and threw him aside. Then the picture broke up.

"What happened?" Spike snapped, but the glitch passed just as Buffy kicked Bobby into rows of pumpkins piled on top of more hay bales.

Bobby scrambled to his feet, but the Slayer never missed a beat and matched him blow for blow. When Bobby threw her against the wagon, the girl didn't falter. She connected with a solid kick, held onto the wagon cover staves, and snagged the vampire in a headlock with her feet. She snapped her legs and flipped him.

"Did you see that?" Spike didn't turn to look at Jacob. He was totally captivated by the gutsy Sunnydale Slayer.

When Bobby tried to grab her, she somersaulted over him, pulled the Halloween calendar countdown sign out of the ground, and jammed the stake into Bobby's chest.

Spike applauded as Bobby vanished in a cloud of dust. "She's got spunk." He paused slightly before turning back to Jacob. "Good job, mate. Now let's see it again."

Spike watched the tape straight through again, and then went back to the beginning to study each individual move. Buffy was quick of mind as well as fast on her feet. She had a natural instinct for hand-to-hand combat that some highly trained men never developed. The challenge excited him as much as it frightened Dru.

"Here it comes." Spike studied the segment where Bobby threw the Slayer against the wagon. "Rewind that. Let's see that again." He moved to another screen and looked back at Jacob. "She's tricky. Baby likes to play."

Jacob didn't comment. He probably couldn't fathom why any vampire would go looking for a fight with a slayer.

That's why I'm the boss, Spike thought as he circled to the third screen to watch a replay of the Slayer staking Bobby with the sign.

"You see that, where she stakes him with that

thing? That's what you call resourceful. Rewind it again." Spike was watching the screens and didn't hear Dru come in.

"Miss Edith needs her tea." Dru held the doll before her as she walked in.

"Come here, poodle." Spike noticed she was shaky on her feet and held out his hand. She hadn't rested long enough to recover from her distress.

"Do you love my insides?" Dru asked. "The parts you can't see?"

"Eyeballs to entrails, my sweet." Spike looked back at the screen. "That's why I've got to study this Slayer. Once I know her, I can kill her. And once I kill her, you can have the run of Sunnyhell and get strong again."

"Don't worry. Everything's switching," Dru said as she walked behind him. "Outside to inside." She paused, her voice low and ominous. "It makes her weak."

"Really?" Spike turned from the screen to look at her. Apparently, a new premonition had shown her something quite different from the one before. "Did my pet have a vision?"

"Do you know what I miss?" Dru lifted her chin in playful defiance. "Leeches."

"Come on," Spike coaxed. "Talk to Daddy. This thing—that makes the Slayer weak, when is it?"

Dru fiddled with Miss Edith and answered hesitantly. "Tomorrow."

"Tomorrow's Halloween," Spike said. "Nothing happens on Halloween."

"Someone's come to change it all." She cocked her head, as though listening to the doll. "Someone new."

Spike usually stayed in on Halloween and watched old monster movies on TV, but he dared not ignore Dru's warning or advice. The Slayer would be weakened tomorrow, and he had come to Sunnydale to kill a slayer.

Sunnydale
September 2002

"You never will," *Dru* said.

Spike knew that. He hadn't killed the Sunnydale Slayer and never would.

"You'll always be mine." *Dru* caressed the side of his face with a phantom touch.

No, he wouldn't. Spike was struck again by the blatant irony. Drusilla, in her madness, delighted in evil. Now that he was insane, there was no pleasure. Only pain. His own.

"You'll always be in the dark with me, singing our lit'le songs." *Dru* traced delicate patterns on his skin, but the fingers that couldn't touch him bored into him. "You like our little songs, don't you?"

Spike tensed. *She* was probing his most secret thoughts, looking for something to yank his chain. *Don't.* He tried, but couldn't stop the violation of his fondest memories.

Early one morning just as the sun was rising . . .

She snatched the lyric and tune, twisted it into a hook, and shoved it into the swamp of his subconscious.

Panicked at the loss of his mother's favorite song,

he reached into the blackwater muck, but it was buried too deep to find.

"You've always liked them," *Dru* said.

What? Spike wondered, disoriented.

"Right from the beginning," *Dru* cooed. "And that's where we're going . . ."

Sunnydale
October 1997

"Why are ghosts white?" Dru asked.

"They're not—except in human imaginations, old movies, and dime-store decorations." Spike lifted the corked bottle of congealing blood Dru had left on the bed table. "What's this?"

"I've been saving it." Dru draped a black cloth over Miss Edith, the last of the dolls to be shrouded for Halloween. "For trick or treats."

"For your play people?" Spike set the bottle down and shrugged into his favorite red shirt.

"Yes, for my lit'le black ghosts." Dru stepped back to study her handiwork. "What tricks shall we play to celebrate this tawdry holiday?"

"You made a rhyme." Spike embraced her from behind and kissed her neck. "You know I wouldn't be going out tonight if I didn't have to work."

"Making the streets safe for the magic man's wee demons and ghouls." Dru bashed one of the dolls in the head with her fist. "Quiet or no sweet stuffing in your pumpkin."

"Magic man?" Spike asked. When he had asked for more specific details about the weakened Slayer, Dru had lapsed back into an agitated hysteria about fire and rotting insides. Her descriptions and interpretations of her visions were often vague, and she resented being pressured. Occasionally, though, important details followed with no prompting. "Is that the 'someone new' who makes everything different?"

"Makes everything real." Dru picked up Miss Edith and closed her hand around the doll's neck, tightening the black cloth. "Don't forget to bring me one."

"A treat?" Spike took his duster off the pipe bracket and slung it over his shoulder.

"Trick-or-treater, pumpkin eater, how does your graveyard grow?" Drusilla turned suddenly, her carefree demeanor darkened by a fearful scowl. "The Slayer's tombstone shimmers. Put her in the ground, Spike—before the winds change."

Spike left the factory through a side exit to avoid the minions. He didn't want to explain why he was breaking with tradition and going out on Halloween. In the long ago past, demons had refrained from moving about on *Samhain* in deference to the spirits of the dead most human cultures honored. As time passed, humanity's respectful observance of All Hallows Eve had been transformed into a grotesque parody with an emphasis on masquerade and panhandling. Vampires, demons, and all other evil entities universally rejected modern humanity's tacky tribute to death and horror. It was a singular matter of honor that all evil shared, and one Spike usually respected by staying in.

But a new and unknown force would weaken the Slayer tonight. Spike no longer cared how he killed her as long as he killed her. Letting Buffy Summers live threatened Dru's health and mocked his Big Bad reputation. Ironically, she would die on All Hallows Eve, the one night of the year she thought she was safe.

As Spike expected, the industrial-district parking lots and alleys were deserted. He headed straight for the Slayer's house; he was a black knife meeting no resistance as he cut through the darkness between factories and warehouses and sped along side streets unlit and little traveled at night. He didn't slow his pace until he hit the bright lights of downtown Sunnydale.

It had been many years since Spike had witnessed the Halloween ritual of trick or treat. The last time had been in 1953, when he had gone into a typical Midwest neighborhood to satisfy his curiosity. Most of the look-alike houses had displayed carved pumpkins lit with candles on their front porches. A few enthusiasts had decorated their lawns with handmade grave markers, cardboard coffins, ghosts, hay bales, bundles of dried corn stalks, and scarecrows. Parents with flashlights supervised children dressed up as pirates, cowboys, princesses, and ballerinas as they went from house to house begging for candy.

Dru had been right. America's postwar Halloween customs were crass and an insult to evil everywhere. The only break in the boredom had been a tall "ghost" in a white sheet, who was stalking two young girls trick-or-treating by themselves. Spike had trailed the ghost, his excitement mounting when the girls realized they were being followed. The older cowgirl had taken the smaller cat-child's hand and hurried her toward a house as the ghost closed in. The children had rushed inside to hide behind a man, who was obviously their father. He hadn't expected the stalker to whip off the white sheet.

"Mommy!" the little girls had shrieked.

Furious at being suckered, Spike would have fed on the whole bloody family if he hadn't promised Dru to abstain because it was the soddin' demons-don't day. On later reflection, he had to admit he admired the ghost mother's subterfuge to protect her young. Besides, that deception was minor compared to how insidiously commercial Halloween had become since 1953.

Spike glanced down Sunnydale's main street, aghast. Every storefront was festooned with decorations that demeaned the symbols of evil and major Bads. Witches, who were often as beautiful as they were powerful, were portrayed as green crones with hooked noses, pointed chins, and warts. Werewolves, zombies, and other mystical monsters were depicted as cute or comical. Every vampire bore a distinct resemblance to Bela Lugosi's Dracula, with wet-combed black hair, sunken dark eyes, pasty white skin, a rouged mouth, and glistening fangs.

Spike detoured onto a side street, but there was no escape from an endless variety of jack-o'-lanterns, black cats, bats, scarecrows, cobwebs, tombstones, ghosts, and goblins. The Party Town costume shop was still open and doing a booming last-minute business. Ethan's, another vendor of Halloween clothes and paraphernalia a few doors down, was closed. Spike sensed something sinister within Ethan's darkened walls, but he had no interest in how other evil entities chose to spend their annual night off.

Once Spike left the downtown business area, the crowds and porch decorations were similar to those he had seen in 1953. The residential neighborhood was overrun with costumed kids being herded from house to house by teenage volunteers or watchful parents. The children's costumes were more elaborate and the themes more varied, ranging from winged fairies and green goblins to sunflowers, doctors, and bunnies.

He moved off the sidewalk into the street to avoid being slowed down in the trick or treat traffic.

"Wow! Cool costume!" A young teenage girl in a gypsy outfit with heavy makeup and gold hoop earrings jumped in front of him. "Who are you supposed to be?"

"Dracula," Spike snapped.

"Don't think so." She peeled a paper off a lollipop. "There's this blond singer—"

"Get lost." Spike snatched the lollipop out of her hand and stuck it in his mouth as he barged past. Any doubts he'd ever had about the wisdom of dropping out on Halloween were dispelled as he navigated the throngs of greedy, giggling children, doting moms and dads, and gushing saps who willingly dished out free candy every year.

Spike couldn't be sure that Buffy would be home. Since Halloween was a night off for the Slayer, too, she was probably out having fun. The Summers' house was the best place to pick up her trail.

Spike paused when he saw an adult "ghost" leading a troop of children toward the house on his left. The long porch was hung with orange paper lanterns, black and orange streamers, and an inflated plastic skeleton. As soon as the elderly lady in residence opened the door, the pint-sized beggars recited their extortion mantra.

"Trick or treat!"

"Oh, my goodness, aren't you adorable!" The woman smiled as she reached into her plastic pumpkin to pay off the trespassers.

For Spike, the ghost was a poignant reminder of times past, evoking a nostalgic pang for the carefree days before Dru had been afflicted, when they had hunted from New York to Seattle at leisure—except on Halloween. He looked away, clearing his mind. He had a slayer to kill.

As Spike started to move on, a wind roared down the street, whipping dead leaves into a frenzied stream and chilling the air. He felt the dark magic roiling on the current and smiled as Dru's words echoed in his mind.

"Someone's come to change it all. Someone new."

"Someone has just cast a monster spell," Spike said, looking back toward the house.

"Oh, dear." The elderly woman stared into an empty plastic pumpkin. "Am I all out? I could have sworn I had more candy."

"Something's happening here, now, isn't it?" Spike watched, fascinated, as the small boy in a red devil cap morphed into a red devil demon with green horns. The old lady didn't realize a slightly taller boy in a green goblin mask was no longer human.

"I'm sorry, mister monster." The woman leaned toward the goblin. "Maybe I'll—"

The goblin snarled and clamped his clawed hands around the old lady's neck. She screamed. The children who had not been changed into monsters screamed and ran.

"No!" The female ghost shouted at the monsters. "Let her go! Stop!"

When the red devil went for the green goblin's throat, he released the woman. She ran back into her house and slammed the door as the two little Bads tried to throttle each other.

"Stop!" The ghost yelled. "What are you doing?"

"Just having a bit of monster rough house." Spike leaned against the rough bark, taking stock of the spell's effects.

A cacophony of terrified shrieks and monster roars reverberated up and down the street. However, not everyone had been affected by the magic. Those that had changed into "the magic man's wee demons and ghouls," as Dru had so accurately put it, immediately attacked those who had not. The two changelings on the porch had been wearing purchased masks and costumes. *From Ethan's?* Spike wondered, remembering the evil he had sensed emanating from the store.

"Stop!" The responsible girl ghost kept trying to break up the fight between the devil and the goblin. "Hey!"

The two little blokes leaped over the porch railing and ran—straight into Spike's clutches. He snagged them both by the collars. "Gotcha!"

Spike held the snarling monsters at arm's length, one in each hand. They kicked and swung at him with short, stubby arms, but it was a futile fight.

"Stop wiggling," Spike ordered. "I'm the boss. Either you're working for me or you're dead. Your choice."

The small demons stopped struggling.

"That's better." Spike patted their heads. "Now just stand there a minute and let me think."

The neighborhood was in chaos. Glass shattered, car alarms blared, and shrieking children ran by, chased by hideous creatures of all shapes and sizes. Farther down the street a man with a gun was taking aim. Then Spike realized the man was Xander, and he was aiming at Willow—wearing short and sassy black leather and burgundy velour.

Spike couldn't hear what the Slayer's friends were saying, but when Xander shouldered his gun and stumbled through Willow as though she weren't there, he knew he had an unexpected problem. Dru had said the magic man would "make everything real." Xander and Willow had obviously been affected by the mysterious transformation spell. He was trigger-happy and armed with real bullets, and she was a ghost. Logically, Spike could assume that the spell would somehow weaken the Slayer, just as Dru had foreseen.

But Dru hadn't seen that Buffy's misfit gang would be transformed as well—into more formidable adversaries. They couldn't seriously hurt him, but they could make killing Buffy a lot harder.

Since the chances of catching the Slayer without her trusty entourage were slim to none, Spike needed backup. There weren't any real demons on the streets to recruit, but the spell-caster, whoever he or she was, had provided him with a handy supply of pseudo-demons.

Motioning the two diminutive minions to follow, Spike headed away from Xander and Willow. The little ones were too small to be much help in a fight, but Ethan's costume store had also catered to adults. Three or four large specimens would fill out the ranks nicely.

The sound of machine-gun fire sent the children diving for cover. They were still mortal and could be wounded or killed. Spike revised his demon recruitment goal to five or six.

The first addition was a pseudovampire Spike shanghaied by the guy's own front door. The dim-wit newbie, in full vamp face, was threatening his hysterical wife, who had the good sense not to invite her deformed and deranged hubby back into the house. Spike promised to help the furious man get even with his wife after he helped Spike get the Slayer.

After that, Spike just had to stand in the street and

choose as the various demons, mutants, and monsters went by.

"Well." Spike grinned as an overweight Sasquatch and two zombies lumbered after two women and an old guy. Sirens wailed in the distance and more shots rang out. Horns honked, things smashed into other things, and a helicopter flew overhead. "This is just— neat."

Despite the underlying seriousness of taking out an incapacitated Slayer, Spike had never dreamed Halloween could be so much fun. The use of magic on the despised holiday was unprecedented, but it wasn't in his nature to complain when someone else's bad worked to his advantage.

Fate was also on his side tonight.

When Spike spotted Cordelia, Xander, and Angel striding down the middle of the street, he waved his recruits into the shadows.

"Are you sure she came this way?" Xander asked. He carried the automatic weapon as though it were part of him. The boy had been playing dress-up soldier and now he was one, with everything in a real soldier's experience and memory at his disposal.

"No," Angel snapped angrily.

"She'll be okay." Cordelia was wearing a striped feline costume, but she was still Cordelia: catty, but not a cat.

"*Buffy* would be okay," Angel shot back. "Whoever she is now, she's helpless. Come on."

Spike turned to his henchmen. "Do you hear that, my friends?"

They growled and snarled, thrilled at the prospect of a brawl.

Spike teased their awakened bloodlust. "Somewhere out there is the tenderest meat you've ever tasted. And all we have to do is find her first."

Chapter Eleven

Spike immediately altered his plan. Vampires could sense the Slayer as surely as they could sense each other. Angel could not tell if Buffy had come this way because he wasn't tracking the Slayer's pungent powers. She had become someone else. Since there was no distinctive Slayer scent to follow, there was no point going to the Summers' house.

Spike followed Angel.

He had enlisted seven demons: a large male vampire, an adult green demon with horns, an adult red demon with horns, and a shaggy-haired child creature, in addition to the red and green monsters and the angry vampire husband. He ordered the recruits to stay a discreet distance back from the trio of Slayer friends. He didn't want to show himself and force a premature confrontation before they found Buffy.

In Sunnydale all things seemed to gravitate to the rundown and abandoned buildings in the industrial district. The transformed Buffy was no different.

As Angel and company moved between two brick buildings, Spike's band of magical makeovers was ambushed. A Frankenstein monster, a medieval black knight, and three small skeletons with sabers swooped out of an abandoned service station. The knight raised his sword and charged Spike.

"I don't have time for this." Spike grabbed the sword and kicked the knight's chest, knocking him off his feet. Clasping the hilt of the sword like a knife, Spike drew the blade back to impale Frankenstein's monster, and Little Red tackled a skeleton. The connected-bones fell in front of Spike, throwing off his aim. The sword went through the padded shoulder of the monster's jacket and pinned him to a warehouse wall. "That works."

The new minions routed the remaining skeletons, passing their bad-guy initiation.

Spike hurried after Angel with his subordinates marching behind, but their delay had allowed the Slayer's friends to vanish in the industrial labyrinth. The warehouse district was a demonic playground, and he couldn't isolate Angel's trail in the thousands of evil essences that permeated the buildings and alleys. He had no choice but to push on, hoping he would stumble across Buffy's rescue squad.

Fate, however, was still playing favorites. Ordinarily

that would have made Spike suspicious and wary, but someone new had entered and changed the rules. As Spike stormed through an empty factory full of large vats and an intricate network of pipes, he saw Willow run past an open delivery door ahead. He sprinted forward, exiting the building just as the girl ghost turned left.

"Got you now," Spike said. "Lead on."

As Spike strode toward the alley, he heard the distinctive sounds of a fistfight. The sharp crack of knuckles on jaw was followed by a loud grunt and the crash of boxes or crates falling.

"Guys!" Willow cried out anxiously.

"Willow!" Xander said.

"Guys, you gotta get inside," Willow said, her voice urgent.

It's a party, Spike thought as he turned the corner and saw his prey: Angel, Xander, Willow, Cordelia, and Buffy. Everyone but the Slayer's Watcher was in the alley. They could run and try to hide, but he had them now.

"We need a triage," Xander said.

"This way," Angel replied, taking charge. "Find an open warehouse."

"Ladies! We're on the move." Xander grabbed his gun as he rushed past Cordelia and Buffy. With Cordelia and Willow following, he led the retreat away from Spike's minion mob.

Angel swept the Slayer into his arms and carried her.

Spike shifted into vamp face, deadly serious now with the odor of fear thick around him. The red- and green-horned demons—economy size and large—growled in eager anticipation as they swept through the alley.

"Over here!" Angel yelled. He stepped back into the light of a security lamp as Xander rushed to open a warehouse door.

As Spike gained on the frantic humans, he saw that the woman in Angel's arms had a mass of long dark hair and was wearing an eighteenth-century ball gown with layers of crinolines. Buffy had been transformed into a compliant and demure colonial lady, the exact opposite of her real identity. He loved the sick trick fate and Dru's unnamed magic man had played on the Slayer and wondered if Angel realized Buffy's getup was intended to attract him, a genuine son of the 1700s.

"Probably not, the dense sod." Spike sneered as Xander slid the warehouse doors open and the humans raced inside.

"Check if there are any other ways in!" Xander shouted and pulled the doors closed as Willow cleared the entrance.

Spike stood back to let his pseudodemons work off some of their energy on the corrugated metal doors. He could hear the people inside trying to reinforce the barrier, but it wouldn't work. Big Green and Hubby Vamp pried the doors open a crack and broke through, rolling barrels and throwing heavy grillwork out of the way.

Spike strode inside ready for action. This Slayer was about to meet her doom.

They found the prey cornered in a large storage area. Spike quickly dispersed his people to subdue Xander and Angel. Willow the ghost was noncorporeal, and Cordelia was a combat zero. Then he turned to Buffy.

"Look at you. You're shaking." Spike advanced on

the sniveling wisp of fluff Buffy had become. "Terri-fied. Alone."

Buffy backed away, whimpering, her cheeks damp with tears.

"Lost little lamb." Spike growled low in his throat, suddenly infuriated by the frightened doe-eyed look on Buffy's soggy face. He struck her across the mouth to wipe the pathetic expression away.

She choked on a startled cry, and her captive friends flinched.

"I love it," Spike said calmly, but that was a lie.

"Buffy!" Angel fought to get free, but Big Red and the second pseudovampire didn't let go.

Spike placed his hand on Buffy's throat. The woman was so terrified she lay down across a piece of metal grillwork without a struggle. She was blubber-ing, too befuddled and intimidated to speak or resist, and that made him angrier. He gritted his teeth and touched the side of her face, his movements slow and deliberate until he grabbed her hair. He tightened his grip, his demonic yellow eyes probing her gaze for a sign that she had once been a vampire slayer, feared throughout the demon worlds.

There was no hint of the Slayer there. The magic man's spell had turned a ruthless demon killer into a helpless, insipid damsel. The difference was too stark to overlook. The weepy twit wasn't Buffy.

Behind him Spike heard Xander break away from the minions and start to fight back.

Spike bared his fangs and flexed his fingers in the girl's dark hair. He could end her life in an instant, but it would be a hollow victory. A fragile, frightened stranger would die in Buffy's body, but he would be deprived of the satisfaction he craved from a slayer kill.

He couldn't do it.

"Now *that* guy you can shoot," Willow said loudly.

Spike braced for the sting of a bullet in the back that never came.

"What the . . ." Xander sounded puzzled.

"I'm scared," a child cried. "I want my mommy." The mysterious spell had been broken, and the henchmen were munchkins again.

Spike looked back, his hand still twined in black hair, and the girl's costume wig came off. He glanced at the hairpiece clutched in his hand and realized that—

Spike snapped his head around as Buffy sat up with a bright smile.

"Hi, honey. I'm home!"

God, I love this one! The thought was barely formed in Spike's mind before the Slayer punched him in the stomach.

Buffy followed with a left to Spike's jaw, then a hard right and a kick that sent him sprawling into a metal staircase. He reached for a length of pipe and came back swinging. Buffy grabbed onto the end of the pipe before it hit her, whipped Spike around, and wrenched the weapon out of his hands. Before he could react, the pipe slid across his face and thudded into his stomach. He doubled over.

"You know what?" Buffy grinned. "It's good to be me." She brought the end of the pipe up under Spike's chin, laying him flat out across the piece of grillwork.

The force of her blow was so great he slid off into a heap on the concrete floor.

Growling, Spike sprang to his feet and faced her. The Slayer met his menacing stare—confident, relaxed, and ready for another go-round.

Spike quickly considered his options. He could fight her, but no one was watching his back except his enemies, a few terrified kids, and four confused and embarrassed men. Besides, she was using a metal pipe, not a stake that could kill him. There was no challenge in continuing a fight that wasn't to the death, but the Slayer could inflict a hell of a lot more pain than he cared to endure.

He ran.

Sunnydale
September 2002

"Right back to the beginning," the *Master* continued. The magnitude of the ancient vampire's power filled every crevice in the storeroom as he stood up.

Spike cowered, overwhelmed.

"Not the bang. Not the word." The *Master's* voice boomed with disdain, inspiring dread. "The true beginning."

Spike rocked forward when the *Master* walked past, as though pulled by the blood bond that flowed from him back through Darla to her powerful sire.

"The next few months are going to be quite a ride," the *Master* went on, "and I think we're all going to learn something about ourselves in the process."

When the old *vampire* turned to glare, Spike shrank from Its contempt.

"You'll learn you're a pathetic schmuck," the *Master* said pointedly, "if it hasn't sunk in already. . . ."

Spike couldn't argue with that.

Sunnydale
October 1997

Spike didn't go straight back to the factory after he left the warehouse district. He ran past the Sunnydale WEL-COME sign into the forest, trying to throw off the fury and frustration that was eating away at his insides. Was that what Dru meant when she warned of the Slayer's poison? That he would be consumed by disgust and self-loathing for his failure? If so, there was an antidote.

Sooner or later he would kill Buffy the Vampire Slayer.

When Spike reached the top of a rise overlooking the town, he paused to peer down. Sirens and car alarms still blared, lingering effects of the transformation spell's chaos. Streets were darkened where lights had been blown out, and tendrils of smoke rose from smoldering fires. All the baby bites were being bundled back into their homes by frightened parents. This was one Halloween they wouldn't forget.

He wouldn't, either.

He should have followed his instincts and not trusted a fate that had made things too easy. Nothing worth doing was easy, and the cosmos was having another soddin' laugh on him. And why not? He was a bloody fool.

He had stalked the Slayer and cornered her, had her right by the throat. He could still feel her racing pulse, the blood pumping through her arteries, the shudder when he touched her skin.

Except that the girl hadn't been the Slayer.

Spike shouted at the night, a scream of savage rage.

He should have killed her anyway, in spite of the false persona, but he didn't.

Because of the terror he had seen in her eyes.

Because they weren't the Slayer's eyes.

Fuming, Spike lit a cigarette. As long as he was being honest with himself, he had a couple more questions he hadn't dared ask.

He had had his hands around Buffy's throat on Parent-Teacher Night, too. He could have snapped her neck in a second, just like he snapped Nikki's. There had been more than enough time before the Slayer's mom clobbered him with the axe.

But he had hesitated.

Why?

What had he seen in the Slayer's eyes then that stayed his hand?

Sunnydale
September 2002

The Slayer's eyes.

The image, startling in its intense clarity, blazed through the fog clouding Spike's mind.

The Slayer's eyes.

"Look at you." The *Master*'s demand was steeped in scorn. "Trying to do what's right, just like her. You still don't get it. It's not about right, it's not about wrong—"

Spike frowned. He heard the words, but they were just words. They weren't even true.

"It's about power," *Buffy* said.

Yes, Spike thought. It was all about power.

"Except you don't have any, Spike. Not anymore." *Harmony* crossed her arms and smiled, smugly, like she always did right before she zinged someone. "The Slayer made you weak. Evil is a lot more powerful than good because evil doesn't care."

Is that true? Spike rolled the concept around in his mind, testing it against all he had been through and thought and felt and learned in a hundred and more years of life and death, of loving and leaving and losing. A rip appeared in the fog, letting another realization slip through. The Other had tried to trick him with a false assumption.

"Tricky bad thing," Spike said, wagging his finger. He folded his arms on his knees and rocked. "Isn't going to work. No more lies."

He remembered the Slayer's eyes.

"Don't think about the Slayer!" *Harmony* stamped her foot, her face a darkening storm. "You were her pet project. She made every day a fresh bout of torture, trying to drive you around the bend, haunting you."

The Other didn't want him to think about Buffy,

but some things were true and some things were false. That was just the way of it.

Spike sensed the important thing skimming across his consciousness, darting back and forth just beyond his grasp, trying to elude the Other that didn't want it known. He stared at the floor, thinking about Buffy's eyes, and the important thing pierced through the mists into consciousness.

Good was more powerful because it *did* care.

That was the power he had seen in Buffy's eyes on Parent-Teacher Night, the first time he hadn't killed her: The Slayer would never give up, but she had been willing to die so good would prevail.

"All the more reason to kill her!" The *Master* railed. "Dead slayers have no power."

"You promised to kill her for princess," *Dru* said.

"You had plenty of chances," *Harmony* reminded him.

Except that Buffy was a force, with a will, strength, and skill that matched his.

Spike stood up, stricken by a truth as profound as his love was pure: Buffy was his equal, and the only person in the world who could give him acceptance and respect that mattered.

"Forget the Slayer," *Dru* said.

Spike stared at the apparition. The Other was strong and still had a grip on his mind, but he knew now what It didn't want him to know. He could fight It, and eventually, he would beat It.

Dru persisted, desperate and sulking. "The Slayer used you, twisted and stomped you, and threw you away—like a toy, battered and broken."

"Buffy needed me to feel alive," Spike said. This truth, crystal clear and immutable, rose from a small patch of serenity embedded in his soul. "And I needed her to feel a man."

That had always been the crux of his life, and now—it wasn't.

Epilogue

Spike waited as Buffy, Giles, and the Potentials left the cemetery, the night's training session having been abruptly adjourned. The Watcher wasn't happy about leaving him behind, but the Slayer understood. Sometimes a man had to be alone.

And for the first time in what felt like forever, he was alone.

The First wasn't showing up as every dead person he had ever known or killed, and all the vengeful voices were silent. He hadn't heard a peep out of them since the primordial source of evil had taken him prisoner, tortured him, and ordered him to choose sides. Spike smiled as he walked by familiar tombstones, still amazed at how easy it had been to tell the First posing as Dru to "get bent."

The door into his old crypt was ajar. He hadn't been back since he left Clem to watch over things while he went off to bargain for his soul. After a while, the flop-eared demon had given him up as gone-for-good and stopped coming by.

Spike kicked an empty vodka bottle as he stepped inside. When the Potentials had asked about his old digs, Buffy had described the crypt as "comfy." Now the place was just trashed. Vandals and thieves had destroyed or taken everything of value. His mattress was gone, the TV screen was shattered, and stuffing had been pulled out through slashes in the chair. When he had stopped living with Dru, he had stopped caring what things looked like as long they worked: chair, lamp, bed, and TV. He hadn't needed much. Now he was content with a cot and shackles in Buffy's basement.

Funny how priorities change, Spike thought, dropping into the lumpy chair. Everything had changed, dramatically and mostly for the better—although not necessarily for his better. He had gone through hell to reclaim his soul only to find out that lost souls come back with hell conveniently built right in.

The spark burned and, since he was a bottomless pit of horrific sin, it probably always would. Still, he didn't have any remorse. Everything he had suffered had been worth it, even if Buffy never let herself love him in that all-consuming, love-of-my-life way that he wanted. He liked to think it was possible. It mattered, just not quite so much now. Buffy had given him something else just as priceless and perhaps even more difficult to earn: Her trust.

The Slayer hadn't jumped to conclusions, assuming he had gone bad when they found out he was killing again. She had looked beyond the evidence to find the truth, that the First had brainwashed him and implanted a trigger. He had memorized the Slayer's words, the words that gave him hope that there was some rhyme and reason for all the pain.

"You faced the monster inside of you and you fought back. You risked everything to be a better man. And you can be. You are. You may not see it, but I do. I do. I believe in you, Spike."

Knowing that Buffy believed in him had helped him withstand the torture and resist the First's evil influence in the caves. But not until tonight had the Slayer shown—beyond all doubt—that her faith in him as a man was absolute. Riley Finn of the Initiative had given Buffy control of Hostile Seventeen's destiny. When the med-lab doctor explained that the chip was degrading and would kill him before long, she had been given a choice: repair it or remove it.

Buffy had removed it.

With the chip's power over him eliminated, the last few pieces of Spike's shattered existence had fallen back into place.

Not very long ago, he had been convinced that Buffy's complete, unconditional trust would validate his worth—just as he had once thought Cecily's affections would. He had been wrong on both counts. He hadn't recognized the truth until tonight, when he was walking away from the Initiative's destroyed complex with his free will restored. He had *always* possessed the courage and strength of character to dance to a different drummer—even as William.

Spike shook his head and laughed quietly, no longer astonished at the ironic turns his long life had taken. As William, he could have put on airs and mimicked the proud gentleman peacocks Cecily so obviously favored. He had thought of doing just that on occasion, but had always rejected the lie. It had been so much harder to be true to himself, to suffer the ridicule and contempt. But that persistent essence, that certainty of who he was, had driven him to find a legend and endure unspeakable torment to get his soul back. He had done that for himself—to be worthy of Buffy.

"That much worked, didn't it?" Rising from the chair, Spike took a last look around. There were memories here, good and bad, but everything was going to change again.

Spike closed the crypt door when he left, putting his past to rest behind him. As he swept through the cemetery, his thoughts turned toward tomorrow and the trials yet to come. Buffy had beaten and killed the übervampire to rescue Spike from the First's caves because she needed a great warrior she could trust: She needed him.

The überbad band was on deck to hit the stage, to take it all down in death and screaming, horror and bloodshed. And that wasn't the raving of a madman.

It *was* coming from beneath to devour.

A chill winter wind rose on the night, stirring dry leaves and howling through mausoleum cracks, stinging his face as though he could be intimidated by an omen. The First had tried to turn his mind to mush, to bury him in the hopeless quicksand of insanity. When that had failed, It tried to break his will with drownings and beatings, but he hadn't broken. And through it all, he had to wonder: Why him?

Spike stopped, suddenly stricken by the rhyme and reason that made sense of his suffering.

The überbad had tried everything in Its arsenal of ultimate power to eliminate him as a warrior because It was afraid of him. If the First—the most powerful evil ever—feared him, and the Slayer—the most powerful force for good—trusted him, then he was the man he had always wanted to be.

Spike moved on, vowing to live up to Buffy's belief in him and his abilities. His had been a noble soul before he lost it. It still was. In the end, he would die to save the world without regret or hesitation— because that was the right thing to do.

ABOUT THE AUTHOR

Diana G. Gallagher lives in Florida with her husband, Marty Burke, five dogs, three cats, a guinea pig, and a cranky parrot. Before becoming a full-time writer, she made her living through a variety of occupations, including equitation instructor, folk musician, and fantasy artist. Best known for her hand-colored prints depicting the doglike activities of *Woof: The House Dragon*, she won a Hugo Award for Best Fan Artist in 1988.

Diana's first science fiction novel, *The Alien Dark*, was published in 1990. Since then, she has written more than fifty novels in several series for all age groups, including Star Trek for middle readers; Sabrina, the Teenage Witch; Charmed; Buffy the Vampire Slayer; The Secret World of Alex Mack; Are You Afraid of the Dark?; and Salem's Tails. Most recently, she co-authored the *Charmed* companion, *The Book of Three*, and *Angel: The Casefiles, Volume 2* with Paul Ruditis.

As many as one in three
Americans with HIV...
DO NOT KNOW IT.

More than half of those
who will get HIV this year...
ARE UNDER 25.

HIV is preventable.
You can help fight AIDS.
Get informed. Get the facts.

www.knowhivaids.org
1-866-344-KNOW

"I'm the Slayer. Slay-er. Chosen One? She who hangs out a lot in cemeteries? Ask around. Look it up: 'Slayer *comma* The.'"

—Buffy, "Doomed"

INTO EVERY GENERATION,

A SLAYER IS BORN

Seven years, 144 episodes, three Slayers, two networks, two vampires with souls(!), two Watchers, three principals, two pigs, one Master, one Mayor, countless potentials: It all adds up to one hit show.

The Watcher's Guides, Volumes 1–3, are the *complete* collection of authorized companions to the hit show *Buffy the Vampire Slayer*. Don't be caught dead without them!

Available from Simon & Schuster

Buffy lives on . . .
in books!

**Stake out a new
Buffy the Vampire Slayer book
every other month!**

Buffy the Vampire Slayer™

Into every generation,
a Slayer is born . . .

Before there was Buffy, there were other Slayers—called to
protect the world from the undead. Led by their Watchers,
they have served as our defense—across the globe and
throughout history.

In these collections of short stories written by best-selling
authors, travel through time to these other Slayers. From
France in the fourteenth century to Iowa in the 1980s, the
young women have protected the world. Their stories—
and legacies—are unforgettable.